DEATH BY SURPRISE

Additional Carolyn Hart Classics

Skulduggery

The Devereaux Legacy

Escape from Paris

Brave Hearts

Castle Rock

CAROLYN HART

DEATH BY SURPRISE

CAROLYN HART CLASSICS

With a New Introduction by the Author

SEVENTH STREET BOOKS™
AN IMPRINT OF PROMETHEUS BOOKS
59 JOHN GLENN DRIVE • AMHERST, NY 14228
www.seventhstreetbooks.com

Published 2013 by Seventh Street Books™, an imprint of Prometheus Books

The characters and events portrayed in this book are fictitious. Any similarity to real persons, living or dead, is coincidental and not intended by the author.

Cover image © Looking Glass/Media Bakery
Cover design by Jacqueline Nasso Cooke

Inquiries should be addressed to
Seventh Street Books
59 John Glenn Drive
Amherst, New York 14228–2119
VOICE: 716–691–0133 • FAX: 716–691–0137
WWW.PROMETHEUSBOOKS.COM

17 16 15 14 13 • 5 4 3 2 1

Library of Congress Cataloging-in-Publication Data

Hart, Carolyn G.
Death by surprise / by Carolyn Hart.
pages cm
ISBN 978-1-61614-869-0 (pbk.)
ISBN 978-1-61614-870-6 (ebook)
1. Mystery fiction. I. Title.

PS3558.A676D445 2013
813'.54—dc23

2013024918

Printed in the United States of America

INTRODUCTION

As a young teenager, I devoured hard-boiled private eye books along with titles by Christie, Tey, Rinehart, Taylor, and Wentworth. I especially remember summer holidays in Long Beach, California. We stayed in a small hotel down by the amusement park and the pier. I walked a few blocks into town to a small second-hand bookstore and bought books by Erle Stanley Gardener, John Creasey, Donald Hamilton, and Jack Iams.

The books were fast-paced, spare, quick.

Death by Surprise is as near that genre as I have ever come. K.C. Carlisle, the protagonist, is a young woman lawyer who has good reason never to quite trust anyone.

When the book was written, young women were just beginning to establish themselves as a force among lawyers. Then law firms occasionally had a woman lawyer. Now women lawyers often comprise a third of big firms and are equally successful in small firms and as prosecutors and defense attorneys.

K.C. is today's independent woman and a perfect match for hidden evil in a twisty tale of greed, manipulation, ambiguity, and a client in deadly peril.

Carolyn Hart

ONE

I glanced down at the legend, K.C. CARLISLE, Attorney-at-Law, in small neat gold lettering near the bottom of the storefront window. I didn't stop and look at it. That wouldn't be cool, would it? My generation is, above all things, cool. But it gave me a thrill. Not that lawyering Carlisles are any kind of oddity, or treat, to La Luz, but it meant a lot to me. I had been among the first wave of women to wash through the nation's law schools. I was K.C. Carlisle, attorney-at-law, and proud of it, still glorying in it after five years of practice, five years of facing down the lady lawyer stereotype. Perhaps that was part of the reason for the kind of law I practiced. But only part. I took almost anything that walked through the door, domestic relations (God, are divorces depressing!), small-time criminal work, wills, mortgages, bankruptcy (and had they been on the increase!), titles, workman's comp., even one malpractice suit. That was the case that proved to me that expert witnesses have a lot in common with call girls. (They strive to please.) I learned a little more every day and by the first anniversary of passing the bar exam, I had gained a lot of confidence in myself and a great respect for our system of law. Inequities happen. Uneven justice occurs. But the law, cumbersome, tedious, and slow, moves forward in its ponderous fashion and more than likely, whatever your complaint, there is a remedy.

I liked looking for remedies. I was on the look out for and took the lead whenever possible in cases fighting incompetence, corruption, exploitation, or prejudice.

I represented Elida Mason Eliot when the school board tried to fire her because she was a lesbian despite her excellent reputation as a teacher. I won.

I represented Ted MacGuire, who was coughing his life away, in a suit against Consolidated Coal, accusing the corporation of moral and legal responsibility for black lung. I lost.

I filed a class action suit against the U.S. Army on behalf of James Morrison and all the other soldiers who watched atomic nimbuses over the New Mexican desert and are now suffering from assorted cancers. No jurisdiction.

I filed another class action for the descendants of the Susquehanna tribe which was summarily and arbitrarily removed from tribal lands, contrary to treaty, relocated in a desert and generally ripped off in the 1880s. That's on appeal to the United States Supreme Court.

I made some enemies. A few old friends of the family studiously looked the other way when we passed on Main Street, but I had a hunch old K.C., for Kenneth Calvin, the first Carlisle to lawyer in La Luz, might have liked my spirit. Kenneth had ridden into town in 1866, a tattered ex-Reb, looking for a new start in the faraway state of California. He hung up a shingle on the second floor of a rickety wooden house at the corner of Main and Mission, and proceeded to represent anybody who asked him. If he had, in the long run, opted more for the railroad and mining interests, you could only say he knew a dollar when he saw one. He had, as a matter of fact, done so well that his offspring still floated at the top of La Luz society, thanks to his acumen.

I unlocked the door and wondered what old K.C. would think if he could see my office. It was as simple as his first had been.

Two straight chairs and my secretary's desk crowded the entry room. I flicked on the overhead light and followed the narrow short hallway to my office door. In a tiny room to the left was my law library. The equally small bathroom was on the right.

I opened my office door, turned on the light, and sighed when I saw my overflowing 'in' box. I looked at the top of the stack. Good. Pat had finished the brief I would file Monday in the Patterson lawsuit, asking damages and a prohibition of further slander of Mabel Patterson's credit by the Central Credit Bureau which had dropped her rating from good to poor because of her divorce. Pat was a marvel and I would be sorry when he finished night law school. He was an excellent typist, an efficient office manager, and quite a bit brighter than I'd assumed an aging halfback could be. He was still a local hero in La Luz, the aficionados remembering the fall Friday seven years past when Pat had run a kick-off back eighty-six yards for a touchdown against archrival Cordova. I had already invited Pat to practice with me and he had smiled wistfully, or as wistfully as anybody his size could, and shaken his head. He had hopes of landing a clerkship with a federal district judge and thereby making a play, after a year, for one of the blue-chip firms. I couldn't fault him for that. There are all kinds of law to practice and each is necessary for the whole to function. I don't have any prejudice against my brethren in the corporate warrens or in the big business firms. I think of us all as worker ants, each carrying his little particle, the end result being the survival of society.

If that seems a little grand, think about it. In *King Richard III,* the conspirators plan first to be rid of all the lawyers. Why? Because they knew their chicanery couldn't survive the law. It's the lawyers who hold us together, keep us apart, and maintain civility. If you don't believe it, imagine for a moment what it would be like without them. It would be back to rule by force and God love you if you're weak, poor, or have something a bigger guy wants.

So I didn't mark Pat as a loss because he wanted to be a corporate lawyer and affluent to boot. I just hoped I could find another secretary as capable as he. And maybe as big. His bulk discouraged the hoods and winos who clustered at the Red Dog Tavern down the street. I had been broken into twice before I hired Pat.

It was a tough part of town, although only two blocks from the glass-encased modern business district, but I didn't want to move. Slowly, gradually, I was becoming known to working class people. They knew where they were on my street. My office, plain and unpretentious, was as much a statement of my practice as the Persian rugs and inlaid flooring were a statement of my cousin Kenneth's.

I was happy as a clam with my surroundings, but I wasn't stupid. I had taken time, when I came in, to shove home the bolt on the front door. It was almost nine o'clock and my street was about as safe as a path in Sherwood Forest after dark. Normally, I avoided coming to the office at night but I needed to check my 'in' box. I had spent the day in court in the little town of Rosemont, a five-hour drive to the north. But I wasn't going to stay long. A quick check of the mail and I would head home to my apartment, a languid swim, a late light dinner and an even more languid nightcap.

Then I saw the unopened letter, propped against my telephone. Pat had appended a handwritten note with a paper clip: 'K.C., I didn't open this. Thought it might be personal. Several matters are ready for sig., see in box. Also, your mother called, wanted call returned, also some dame (youngish sounding) called four times, wouldn't leave name. See you Mon. Pat.'

My mother had called? How odd. How decidedly odd.

I pulled off the note, saw the letter's face, and was automatically irritated. Yes, it would be personal and I knew who wrote it. That infuriating prig, my dear cousin Kenneth. Kenneth Calvin Carlisle the Vth, for God's sake. Which made him think he could be the only K.C. Carlisle in town. That was why he addressed the letter to Miss Katharine Cecilia Carlisle. Only Kenneth wrote to me as Katharine Cecilia. Kenneth and the IRS. But to everyone else, I was K.C. (the accent on the K, as in Kay-cee) Carlisle. It was my name and I had as much right to it as anyone else. And, if you wanted to split legalities, it was my father who was Kenneth Calvin Carlisle IV, not Kenneth's. Kenneth's father was Robert, a younger brother of my Dad's. So I thought it quite unjustified when Kenneth almost came unglued, in a gentlemanly fashion, after I passed the bar and opened up a law office as K.C. Carlisle.

Who else should I open it up as? I had demanded irritably. Besides, his clients shouldn't have any trouble telling us apart since his offices were on posh Durango Street and he dangled a Roman numeral after his name. It didn't pacify Kenneth.

So I asked why didn't he practice as Kenneth C. Carlisle V. After all, he went by the name Kenneth. I was the one known as K.C.

It would destroy the tradition, he replied querulously.

That, I said silkily, was just too bad. Besides, I would have bet my last *Reporter* that the original K.C. would have felt a lot more comfortable in my office with my clients than he would in the sumptuous decorous suite of offices where Kenneth and his partners cosseted their very rich clients.

The quarrel over our name was just another in a long series of disagreements. Name a topic. Put Kenneth on one side and me on the other.

I ripped open the letter.

Dear Katharine:

The beneficiaries of the Cochran-Carlisle Trust will meet at 4 p.m. Monday in my office to vote upon dissolution of the trust as suggested by Priscilla Carlisle. The trustee, La Luz National Bank, has agreed to authorize dissolution upon a majority vote of approval by the beneficiaries. You will recall that the trust became eligible for dissolution upon the date when all beneficiaries had reached the age of 25.

Very truly yours,
K.C. Carlisle V

cc: Priscilla Carlisle
Edmond Carlisle
Travis Carlisle

I sat down in the old creaky chair that had once belonged to the original K.C. Carlisle. He had succeeded as a lawyer but it was his grandson, K.C. III, who really raked it in. Mining, railroading, shipping. If it made a profit, he had some. And, like most of the very very rich, he didn't cotton at all to the idea of sharing his spoils with the government when he breathed his last. So he made huge gifts to family members and, finally, salted away what was then a tidy two million in a trust with the principal subject to distribution only upon all of the grandchildren reaching the age of twenty-five.

Priscilla, Kenneth's younger sister, turned twenty-five a week ago.

Now, according to this letter from Kenneth, Priscilla wanted the trust opened.

That I didn't believe.

Not that Priscilla didn't love money. She did and she spent it like water washes over Niagara. But Priscilla has the brains of a woolly angora. She would think a trust had something to do with the afternoon soaps. She never had an original thought in her life.

Somebody had put her up to it.

That left Kenneth, Edmond, and Travis. Edmond is my oldest brother and his conservatism is as pervasive as my liberalism. He is a grey forty and adding up his coupons must be his biggest pleasure. He and his wife belong to a local chamber music group and take birdwatching tours.

Edmond's income is high. He has a touch of old K.C. III's moneymaking skill. For that reason, he would be appalled at a dissolution, for his portion of undistributed trust income would be taxed on his tax rate.

The trust had been restricted to distributing only twenty per cent of the income earned annually. There would be a ton of money to be taxed although the principal was tax-exempt, of course. But the corpus had more than quadrupled in recent years, the trustee having had the wit and, I'm sure, the luck to get heavily into the gold market. That was back when the luscious metal sold for $41 an ounce. You know what it sells for now. It had always seemed to me to be a bit un-American but none of the other beneficiaries had any trouble with that.

I didn't actually think about the trust too often. But I remembered every quarter when a substantial check arrived. They made the difference between stop and go, my first few years in practice. This last year I had eked out a modest profit. But I could never have afforded my apartment, sauna, Jacuzzi and microwave oven, without that extra. Or my car. I knew too that there was a contradiction in a storefront lawyer driving a Porsche. Or perhaps not. The best of all worlds.

But I had never thought about dissolving the trust at the earliest possible moment and getting my hands on that kind of money. And my portion of the undistributed income would be taxed only at the modest rate of my regular income.

I did some rough, very rough calculations. Each beneficiary would come out with about four million. Wow!

Edmond would oppose dissolution, of course. How about Travis? Travis is my second brother. He teaches East Asian art at the University of Chicago and if anyone ever suffered from compulsive collectomania, it is Travis. His apartment rivals the Oriental Institute. If the trust were dissolved, he could buy and buy and buy.

I couldn't imagine Travis working through Priscilla. I suppose they passed in the halls at Christmas but that would be the extent of their communication.

No, it wasn't Travis in the prompter's box.

It damn well had to be Kenneth. And that was a shocker.

Kenneth was as conservative as Edmond, as prudent as the Bank of America, and as cautious as a Baptist preacher at an ecumenical breakfast.

Besides, Kenneth too would lose money on the undistributed income because of his high tax-bracket.

What could prompt Kenneth to favor dissolution? Could it be his political campaign? He had won handily the Republican nomination to run for the House seat for our District, but he was in a hot and heavy contest with Greg Garrison, the Democratic nominee. So far, the polls showed them neck and neck, but, if anything, Kenneth was favored as the District had gone heavily Republican in the last two general elections.

But how could Kenneth need money? He had plenty. He had an extremely lucrative tax practice, the income from the trust, and a very wealthy wife. If he really needed money, he had only to ask Megan. Her fortune made the Carlisles look like ne'er-do-wells.

Of course, with Megan's money always available, I guessed that she and Kenneth lived his income to the hilt, a summer home in Carmel, a 27-foot yacht, weekends in New York to see the plays, two Mercedes. In short, whatever they fancied, they had. As Greg had said bitterly, in his campaign, the Carlisles just wanted to go to Washington, D.C., to join the social scene, not to represent the District. Kenneth smiled at the attack and suggested that as much is accomplished at dinner parties in Washington as on the House floor and he and Megan were quite well equipped to represent his constituency either place.

So it didn't make any sense to think that Kenneth had put Priscilla up to trying to dissolve the trust. Did Priscilla have a new boy friend, one with avid intentions? I would have to find out.

Then I yawned, too tired to care what happened to the trust or Kenneth or Priscilla or any of them. I mean, what difference did it make to me?

Well, it might put quite a huge sum of money at my personal disposal. I had ambivalent feelings about money, as everyone does, perhaps. I hated equating money with worth. I knew, from the most personal of experience, that wealth doesn't reflect anything except a particular talent, that of making money. And, too often, it was a talent of some forbear, not the present possessor, who might not have the wit to earn a subsistence if thrust into the world without a penny. I liked the idea of everybody starting fresh. The inheritance taxes make a feeble attack on inherited wealth, but, believe me, the ultra rich, with the able assistance of clever tax-lawyers, stay that way, generation unto generation.

But I didn't have to think about it right this minute. I reached over, marked the time of the meeting on my calendar, then riffled quickly through the stack of papers in the 'in' box. At the bottom was a copy of the morning paper, the La Luz *Beacon.* I had left early. It was a long drive to Rosemont, so I hadn't read today's issue. I looked at the front page in irritation. There it was again, another editorial touting Greg Garrison and berating Kenneth. It was almost enough to drive me to support my cousin. The *Beacon's* attacks came as no surprise. The *Beacon* always opposed the Carlisles on any front. It was owned by the Nichols family. The Nichols and the Carlisles did not socially interact. It could be an awkward fact sometimes in a city the size of La Luz. You did not invite a Nichols and a Carlisle to the same party. It had always been thus, since before I was born as far as I knew. I didn't know why. Mother and Dad always sloughed away my questions, responding vaguely that old man Nichols and Uncle Bobby had hard feelings. They were both dead now but the *Beacon* apparently didn't know it. If it hadn't been for Greg, I would have rallied to Kenneth even though I was a Kennedy Democrat.

But there was Greg. He was just a little older than I. He was handsome, tough, and the most exciting person I had ever known. Greg was District Attorney when I had my first criminal case. My client, Tommy Wallace, was accused of holding up a convenience store. The clerk identified him. Greg had a reputation as a tough prosecutor on this kind of case. Too many hoods high on drugs had killed too many clerks along the Coast in recent years. But Tommy's older sister believed he was innocent. She patiently placed ads in small town papers up and down the coast and talked the radio station into repeating free her query, "If you gave a ride on Highway 101 on the early morning hours of Aug. 14, 1978, from Laguna Beach to Santa Barbara to a young man with blond hair and a tattoo on his right arm, please come forward to prevent a miscarriage of justice." Tommy had claimed he was hitchhiking during the hours the robbery was committed. A Robert Michaelson of Santa Barbara heard the plea and responded. The jury believed him so Tommy was acquitted. After the case was over, Greg spoke to me on the way out of the courtroom. "Congratulations, Counselor. I don't run into many Perry Mason endings. How about a cup of coffee?"

That was the beginning of a hectic friendship. Greg assumed that I remembered him. We had gone to the same high school. I didn't, frankly. He had been from the wrong side of town, a poor boy who worked after school for money, not fun, and didn't have the time to play sports. So the boys with money and time were on the football team. Like Kenneth.

"Big deal," Greg said once, bitterly. "Macho football player. Hell, I could take Carlisle with one hand."

"I suppose there is a lot of hand-to-hand combat on the House floor," I responded drily.

Greg glared, his eyes hot and angry. "He's always had everything.

Well, I'll tell you one thing, K.C., his money isn't going to buy this election for him."

Damn the election. Well, at least it would soon be over.

The *Beacon* headline announced:

CAMPAIGN TO CLIMAX WITH DEBATE

The *Beacon* was sponsoring a debate between Greg and Kenneth a week from tonight in the high school auditorium. I glanced at my calendar. The debate would be on Halloween evening. I wondered if the voters would be amused. Trick or treat. But it wouldn't be a laugh-filled program to me. It promised to be a harsh confrontation. Greg would want me there, prominently on his side.

I sighed. I didn't like to be pushed. And I was tired. Too tired tonight to sit around thinking about Greg and Kenneth and the Cochran-Carlisle Trust. Tomorrow. As Scarlett, one of life's survivors, knew full well, you can handle anything . . . tomorrow.

I began to restack the papers then stopped to listen. Yes, that was the rattle of the front door knob. The door was locked, of course, locked and the dead bolt shot home.

The handle rattled again then a loud knock reverberated. I hesitated. The knock sounded again. I didn't like the flutter of fear in my chest but I also don't like the rape statistics in our fair coastal city. I reached down, opened the shallow right front-drawer and picked up the .22 pistol Greg had given me after the second break-in of the office. I tucked the gun in the waistband of my skirt, beneath my beige linen blazer, and walked out into the front office.

TWO

Someone stood in the darkness beyond the front door. I felt terribly vulnerable. The plate glass storefront window and the plate glass of the door made too much glass altogether. Plate glass shatters like pop bottles. Maybe I should put up bars like the pawnshop next door. It would be like living in a cage, but safer, much safer.

The door handle rattled.

The little sigh of relief I gave when I saw my caller was a woman was immediately followed by a surge of irritation. I looked down at my watch. It was almost ten o'clock. Why on earth would anybody knock on a lawyer's door at this hour of the night? But, of course, there were many possible reasons, somebody in jail, a battered wife, a DUI, or what the police delicately describe as a domestic disturbance.

I slid back the bolt and opened the door.

"Yes?"

"I want to talk to you." She said it crisply, her voice low, clear, and self-possessed.

This wasn't the usual late night emergency. This was something different, something totally out of the ordinary.

I had a quick impulse to shut the door.

"My office hours are nine to five weekdays and ten to two on Saturdays."

"It won't wait." There was a curious tone to her voice. A hint of threat?

"Sure it can." Antagonism flared between us. I started to close the door. She moved quickly, jamming her purse between the door and jamb.

"Oh yes, Miss Carlisle, you will see me—if you value your family name."

It should have been funny, something out of a 1905 melodrama. Who, for God's sake, talked in terms of family name anymore?

It wasn't funny.

"What do you mean?"

"That's better." The tone was soothing and as rude as a slap. "Let me in and I'll tell you all about it."

I wanted to slam the door, but I wanted more to know who she was, what she was up to. A lawyer picks up some useful skills. If you take enough depositions, you learn a cardinal rule of interviewing—get them talking. It's amazing how people will reveal themselves if you give them enough rope.

"You're sure you have the right person?" I asked.

"Oh yes, Miss Carlisle."

I let her in, relocked the door, and led the way to my office.

She was about my age and quite beautiful in a sleek, high-rise fashion. There are high-class hookers in LA who have her look, shiny and all-American, like Iowa cheerleaders, but with an overall gloss that is unmistakable. Her blond hair glistened like spun gold, her eyes were lake blue, and her profile quite perfect. The only odd note was in the look she gave me, intent, speculative, and hostile. Then she glanced around my office. She brushed past me to run her hand under the center drawer.

"Hey . . ." I began.

"Relax, Miss Carlisle. I'm just making sure you don't trigger a little black recorder when your clients start to talk."

"I assure you," I began stiffly.

"Oh, come off it, honey. All the in people do it. But I guess you are just getting started."

The implication, of course, was that I was a square-toed rube, dewy-eyed and dumb.

"You must," I said softly, "keep charming company."

"Yes. Charming as hell." She dropped onto the chair that faced my desk, fished a spiral notebook and a ballpoint out of her purse, and a pack of cigarettes. She began to open it. "Don't mind if I smoke, do you?"

She had the cigarette out as I replied, "Yes, I do."

She gave me a level look and dropped the package back into her purse. "My, aren't we something. Rich, beautiful, and hygienic."

I folded my arms. "It's late. The office is closed. What do you want?"

She flipped open her notebook. "Okay, Miss Carlisle. Your father was Kenneth Calvin Carlisle IV. Right?"

"Just a minute. You have an advantage over me. Who are you?"

She raised an eyebrow. "I thought you probably knew. I suppose the family grapevine hasn't gotten to you yet. I'm Francine Boutelle and I'm writing a story about the Carlisle family. For *Inside*

The family grapevine. If it existed, I wasn't plugged in. I spent as little time as possible, quite frankly, dallying with my family. When Dad died, I felt cut adrift. I had not realized until then that it was he who meant family to me. The rest of them . . . but that was no business of Francine Boutelle's so I just looked bland.

"I shouldn't think," I said mildly, "that *Inside Out* would be interested in the Carlisles."

"Spoken like a true daughter of the rich. Honey, there's nothing a magazine such as *IO* appreciates more than people like the Carlisles. You've been rich forever. You run La Luz. And there's a lovely luscious hint of scandal popping out all over."

So she intended some kind of slimy article on us. Nothing that appeared in *Inside Out* would surprise me. It was a cheap magazine, pandering to the public's lust for scurrilous exposes. It loved to parade as a crusading journal. One recent issue featured an article on private play days at public expense, i.e., a detailed description of a city manager's hijinks at a government seminar in Las Vegas. He lost his job, his wife filed for divorce, and he was indicted for false travel expenses. As a citizen, I don't like to be had, but it seemed to me he paid a pretty stiff penalty for one rousing weekend. But, as the magazine worried, Who Knew How Many Other Ill-gotten Gains There Had Been? Another issue focused on an LA banker's wife with a weakness for quarterbacks (she liked to help them out to the tune of several hundred a month, poor boys), and the NCAA was now in the midst of a full-blown investigation that threatened to balloon into an all-out recruiting scandal with the resulting sanctions sure to ruin some coaching careers and cripple the University team for several seasons.

I wondered how Ms. Boutelle thought she could find enough juicy tidbits to make the Carlisles competitive? There was always Uncle Bobby, of course, Kenneth's father. But Uncle Bobby was dead and it couldn't be too exciting to go after him.

"Why do you want to talk to me?"

"You were very close to your father, Judge Carlisle."

I frowned. *Inside Out* didn't spend much time exploring civic virtue. By no means. It concentrated on frailty, fraud, and deceit.

Of all the Carlisles, past or present, my father had been the finest. He was honorable, decent, fair.

"What about my father?"

"I want to get your view of him, as a man and a judge. It makes a story more real to the reader when you can include intimate details. You know the kind of thing, the day I turned sixteen and what my father said to me, that kind of thing."

"I admired my father very much," I said slowly. "He was an honorable man."

She tilted her head to one side. "Now that's interesting, that really is. So he had you fooled, too."

For a moment, I really couldn't believe what I had heard. Then I was furious. I was so angry I could scarcely see. When I could trust myself to speak, I said harshly, "Get out of here. Now."

"Wait a minute," she said quickly, "I can tell we have a lot to talk about. I want . . ."

I stood. "Get out."

She looked down at her notebook and began to write furiously.

I reached out to the telephone. "Get out now or I'm going to call the police."

She ignored me, wrote for a moment longer, then snapped shut the notebook. "Okay, Miss Carlisle. I'll be on my way. But we could have a very interesting chat. About the Levy case."

The Levy case. I remembered it, of course. You don't forget the cases that touch people you know. Dad had been criticized because he didn't disqualify himself, but he was no great friend of the Levy family. He knew them. In a small town, the rich all know each other, but there was no intimacy so Dad sat and heard the evidence accusing Adolphus Levy of fraud and stock misrepresentation. Ultimately, Dad accepted a negotiated plea and sentenced Levy to a year in prison. Dad then suspended the sentence, citing Levy's heretofore unblemished record and the court's feeling that the misrepresentation had been primarily a matter of poor judgment, not malicious intent.

It was the kind of case that could have gone either way. Another judge could have looked at the same evidence, seen no mitigating circumstances, and assessed the maximum penalty, ten years in prison.

But Adolphus Levy had a good reputation and even the *Beacon,* with all the bad blood between the Nichols and the Carlisles, had commended Dad for the sentence in a short, stiffly written editorial.

"The Levy case has been around for a long time," I said wearily. "It's a dead horse."

"I've done a lot of research on the Levy case, honey, and I've got the goods. It isn't just a matter of judicial propriety, either. No, ma'am. It's fifty thousand bucks in a bag."

"Nonsense," I said sharply. My perspective righted. This girl with the beautiful face and vulgar speech seemed absurd now. Perhaps Dad could have been criticized for his decision, but he couldn't have been bribed. Never. Not in a million years.

"Not nonsense," she said softly. "The bag man was Sonia Levy's nephew, Albert Gersten, and he delivered the money to the Carlisle lake front home on Thanksgiving night, 1975."

"No."

She shrugged. "I'm really sorry, honey, but it's true. I know all about it. Albert Gersten's ex-wife told me and I've got it on tape."

For the first time, a little sliver of fear touched me like early frost on a windowpane. It wasn't true. It couldn't be true. I would never believe it.

Her dark blue eyes watched me avidly.

"I don't care if you've taped the archangel Gabriel. It isn't true."

"Oh yes, it is. I even have the serial numbers of the bills."

I felt angry again. How tawdry. How demeaning to Dad. "Look, Ms. Boutelle, I don't care what you have. I'll never believe my father was a crook. So let's call it a night."

"Wouldn't you like to hear the tape? See what kind of proof I have?"

For the first time, it occurred to me that, cheap magazine or not, this wasn't quite the obvious course for an interview. Of course, I was tired, but still, it shouldn't have taken me so long to tumble.

"Why should I care about your sources?" I asked slowly. "I've told you it can't be true. I suppose my father had enemies. All judges make enemies and some of them might be willing to say anything, now that he is dead and can't answer. But you won't convince me, no matter who you quote."

She forced a smile, tried to look ingratiating. But her eyes were still cold and avid.

"Look, Miss Carlisle, I'm always open to persuasion. I want to give both sides."

"There aren't two sides. My father wasn't a crook."

She gave a little sigh. "It's so hard, especially for a free-lance writer. You get started on an article and it turns out to have all kinds of ramifications. And, of course, you don't get paid a penny until you turn in the completed manuscript. It's expensive, doing so much research. Really, you wouldn't believe how much it costs."

I leaned back in my chair. Now my eyes must have been as cold as hers.

"How much?"

She ignored the bald question.

"If you want to help finance my research," she began.

"How much?"

"It would all depend, of course. Any substantial aid would give you some kind of rights in deciding what would be printed."

"Sure. How much?"

"About $50,000."

I doodled across the top of my legal pad, making fat round zeroes in a sturdy line.

"Even with inflation, that's quite a bit for a blackmailer."

"Blackmail." Her voice oozed shock. "You've misunderstood me, Miss Carlisle. We are talking . . . oh, more along the lines of an investment."

"An investment?"

"Yes. An investment in the future of your family's good name."

"I see." I pulled open my desk drawer, dropped my pen in it. "This has all been very interesting, Ms. Boutelle, but you've called on the wrong Carlisle. To begin with, I'm not worried about my family name. Moreover, I don't have $50,000 so this is quite an academic discussion."

"But you will have."

I looked at her sharply.

She said it quickly, confidently. I could see the edge of the cream-colored envelope from Kenneth in my 'in' box.

"I will? What do you know about my finances that I don't, Ms. Boutelle?"

"The trust," she snapped impatiently. "You'll have all the money in the world when the trust is dissolved." She breathed it with lingering delight. "I could have asked for a lot more."

Get them talking. It always reveals more than they know. Sure, she could have asked for more. And she would. If anybody ever paid her once, she would see it as a gold-plated source of income, continuing income. But colder than that came the realization that she must indeed know a very great deal about the Carlisles. I had not known the trust might be dissolved until this evening. How had Francine Boutelle known?

"You seem to know a great deal about my family," I observed.

"Oh, I do," she said with great satisfaction. "Yes, I do. Lots, Miss Carlisle. About you and your father and your cousin Kenneth and his father and about Priscilla and your brothers, Edmond and Travis."

I laughed. A tired laugh but a real one. "You know more than I or anybody else would ever care to know, Ms. Boutelle. Now, it's been interesting talking to you, but, as I said earlier, I'm tired. More than that, I'm bored with it. As far as I'm concerned, you can write until your fingers turn to bloody stumps and I won't read what you've written or care."

"Not even if it's about your mother?"

My mother. The paragon of virtue. The exemplar of *noblesse oblige.*

"If you have something on Grace," I said drily, "you're quite clever."

I pushed back my chair and stood, obviously waiting for her to leave. She gave it one last shot.

"I have proof, Miss Carlisle. About your father. About all of them."

"Gracious, did they all get $50,000 in the dark of night at the lake house? It must have been quite crowded, bagmen coming and going."

For the first time, a flush rose in her face. "Okay, Miss Carlisle. If you think it's so damned funny, I'll be on my way."

"No, I don't think it is especially funny. Do you think you can blackmail me with innuendoes about my family? You don't have proof or you would have it with you, whatever 'it' could be. All you have is gall. I should call the cops right now. I really should. I won't this time, but if you ever say anything like this publicly or print it, I'll file suit against you for libel and I'll lodge a complaint of attempted blackmail. You don't have anything on the Carlisles—and you never will."

She stood and she was angry, too. "Don't I? You try me, Miss Carlisle. And you haven't even asked what I'm going to put in about you."

No, I hadn't asked. I wouldn't ask. Probably she had found out about Toby. But I didn't care. I had made no secret of him at the time.

"No, I haven't asked. I'm not interested. All I want is for you to leave. Now."

She jammed her notebook into her purse. "You're so sure of yourself, aren't you? Little Miss Rich Bitch. Don't you think everyone will enjoy reading about Sheila and how she really died?"

My shock must have shown on my face because abruptly she looked triumphant and pleased. "Did you think no one knew outside of the family?"

I should have expected it. When she first began to talk, I should have foreseen that it would come, the question of how Sheila died. But I had buried my memory of that day so deep, I had pushed that memory into a recess of my mind. I never thought of Sheila. Never. I stood mute, facing the slender lovely girl with the brutal words.

But perhaps she wasn't so perceptive, after all. As if from a great distance, I heard her words bombarding me, trying to break through what she judged to be indifference.

"So you're too good even to talk to me? Do you think I'm bluffing? About any of it?"

"I don't care," I said dully.

"You'd better care, Miss Carlisle. Or everyone will know all about you and the rest of the Carlisles, know just how phony that self-righteous front is."

"I don't care." I didn't. Not about her or what she said, not even about the rest of the family. None of it mattered compared to the great throbbing wound she had reopened with that one awful sentence: *Don't you think everyone will enjoy reading about Sheila—and how she really died?*

"I'll give you one chance," she said venomously, "just one, Miss Wonderful Carlisle. You can come to my apartment Wednesday night. At eight. I'll have the manuscript there and you can see how much it might be worth to you not to have it printed. I suggest you bring with you the sum of money we mentioned."

She pulled out her notepad, scribbled on a sheet, tore it out, and flung it on my desk.

I followed her to the front door and let her out. We didn't speak another word.

Back in my office, I picked up the sheet of paper and read the address, 1700 Camarillo Rd., Camarillo Apts., Apt. 14-D.

I crumpled the sheet into a ball and flung it into the waste-basket.

Sheila.

I had not thought about her for years. Whenever I saw a little girl that age, about ten with long blonde hair and gentian blue eyes, I would turn away and think of the moment, of the weather, of the sounds of traffic in the street, of the angular shape of shadows on concrete. I would not think of Sheila. I shivered though my office wasn't cold and clutched the back of my chair, clung to it, my knuckles white with strain. I felt dizzy, sick.

I would not think of Sheila.

All my defenses against the world wavered, my image of myself as unruffled, competent, and in charge.

The phone rang.

It rang again.

Slowly, stiffly, I reached out and picked up the receiver. "Hello." My voice came from far away. "Hello," I said it again, louder, clearer, pushing away the image of Sheila, closing my mind, refusing to remember.

"K.C.?"

I knew who it was, of course. Just the sound of my name and I knew. The memory of Sheila had always been strongest around Mother. But I had had practice in barring Sheila from my mind when I saw Mother, years and years of practice. It made it easier once again to push memory away.

"K.C., I called earlier. Your . . . secretary said you would be in late tonight."

Every word she said helped, made it possible for me once again to be K.C. Carlisle in a world of my own creation. It was typical of Grace to pause before she said secretary. She thought it quite improper for a woman lawyer to have a male secretary. It was just one more proof of my bohemianism. I could almost laugh then, safely back in my familiar world. Only the odd chance of talking to Grace could have prompted that descriptive phrase.

"Yes," and I managed to say it pleasantly, strongly, "I just got back. A case in Rosemont."

"That is a long drive."

"Yes."

All the months of separation hung between those short stilted sentences. How long had it been since I had talked to Grace? Dad died eighteen months ago. I had seen her last Christmas at Edmond's.

Why had she called?

I thought we long since had said all there was to be said between us.

"I have invited your brothers and your cousins for dinner Monday night. I would like for you to come."

I wanted to say, hell, Grace, you don't sound like you want me. You never have wanted me. Don't you remember, Grace, I'm the one without any character?

When I didn't answer at once, she continued, her voice sharpening. "K.C., it is quite important. A family council."

A family council. I knew Grace's standards were a survival from another era. Are we excommunicating someone? I wanted to ask. But I didn't. Because, for the first time in all the years I had known my mother, I heard an appeal for help.

"What's wrong?"

She hesitated. I shouldn't have been so direct. Had I scared her off?

"It's quite a terrible thing, an awful thing, actually."

"Mother, what is it?"

"Perhaps, if we all stand together, make it clear there will be reprisals. We could even threaten to buy that dreadful magazine."

So Francine Boutelle had frightened Grace.

"I wouldn't worry, Mother," I said reassuringly, "there are libel laws. She will have to be very careful what she writes."

"But if she can prove . . ." Grace's voice was faint, thinned by fear.

"Well, truth is a defense against libel, of course. What is she bothering you about, Mother? Is it the Levy case?"

Mother gave a little moan. "Oh, K.C., I just don't know what to do."

It shocked me. Could Francine really have something on Mother? Lordy, Lordy.

"Mother, there's no sense in being frightened. Tell me what's she's threatened."

"K.C., something has to be done." I could hear the capital letters. It was her imperious voice, a voice I particularly detested.

"Unfortunately, it's a free country," I said drily. "She can publish and tell us to be damned. Unless, of course, we are willing to pay her off, and keep on paying, ad infinitum."

"Perhaps that's what we shall have to do."

"I shouldn't think Dad would like that."

"I don't know what to do. Oh, I don't know what to do." It was as near a plea as I'd ever heard from Grace.

"Look, Mother, there's a limit to how much crap—"

"K.C."

The reprimand was automatic. It almost cooled my resolve to help. But she couldn't change what she was. And she was, after all, my mother.

"Sorry, Mother. Anyway, Boutelle can't put anything too hideous in her story unless she has the facts to back it up. But I'll come to your pow-wow. Maybe we can do something."

"K.C.," and for the first time in many years, there was a hint of warmth in her voice to me, "I appreciate it. I knew you would come. You . . . in some ways, you are very like your father. Nothing ever frightens you. And he always knew how to solve things."

"I'll do my best," I said gently. "About seven then? Monday? At . . . home?"

"Yes."

"Who's coming?"

"Everyone," she said simply. "Travis will be in town for the trust meeting Monday afternoon and he and Lorraine will be staying here."

After I put down the phone, I looked thoughtfully at my 'in' box and the edge of Kenneth's letter. So Mother knew about the trust meeting. I began to see why the meeting was going to occur.

As for the dinner, it would be quite a dog-and pony show. 'Everyone' included quite a raft of Carlisles, Kenneth and his wife, Megan; Priscilla; Edmond and Sue; Travis and Lorraine, Grace and me.

It would be a long evening.

THREE

I wanted to ignore the phone. I pulled the pillow over my head but I still could hear the infuriating ring. Abruptly, I was awake. I rolled over, picked up the receiver.

"H'lo."

"K.C., I called and called yesterday."

It wasn't much to say but the sound of his voice caressed me.

"Greg."

"Did I wake you? I'm sorry. Sorry it was by phone. I'd rather be there."

"Mmmh."

"K.C., when are you going to decide?"

"Now his voice was deeper, softer, compelling.

"I don't know. Not before breakfast."

A pause, then he sighed. Finally, he laughed. "Are you never serious? You make it tough on a man."

Greg was pressing me, pressing too hard. And once again, I was slipping free, keeping my distance. Yet I was attracted to him, more so than to anyone since Toby. But marriage? It was such a final, irrevocable act. At least it was in my view, notwithstanding the statistics on today's marriages, wed in haste, divorce at leisure.

"I'm going to campaign up the coast this weekend. Come with me."

I knew what he meant, what he offered.

This, frankly, was what I had expected to happen with us and to us since we first met. We both knew it. There was an excitement when we were together when his hand touched mine, when we stood close. He was the one who held back and, to my discomfiture, began to talk of marriage. I might be ready for an affair, but I wasn't ready for marriage.

What had changed his mind? Did he think that seduction might lead to wedlock?

"It's beautiful," he said softly. "A friend has loaned me his cabin. It overlooks the ocean."

"With moonlight and violins, it would be a zinger."

"Come with me."

I wanted to. I wanted to very much.

"I'd like to, Greg," I said softly. I heard his quick intake of breath so I continued hurriedly, "But I can't. I have some things I must see to this weekend. Family things."

"What's wrong?"

So he already knew me well enough to hear the unease in my voice.

I almost told him, almost spread out the Carlisles' woes for his inspection. But he was, after all, running against my cousin. That didn't mean he would try to capitalize on a general diatribe against the family. Still, and it was a little fuzzy in my mind, it wasn't any of Greg's business. At least, not yet. So I diverted him.

"Oh, one thing and another. I have to talk to John Solomon on a case. A rush deal."

"Oh."

If I loved him, the flat monosyllable implied, I would fling all ties to the winds and race to his side.

"There will be other weekends," I offered.

"Sure."

"How's everything coming?"

I was a little ashamed of myself. There is nothing like punching the right button. He started off grudgingly but by the second sentence his voice was vibrant with excitement. I listened absently, ". . . and the polls show I'm gaining . . . have 12 rallies planned . . . even some Republican support and that'll scare Carlisle, and . . ."

He was in high good humor by the time I wished him luck on his jaunt up the coast.

"Call me when you get back."

"I will," he said happily. "First thing. K.C., I'll be thinking of you."

When you aren't thinking of the campaign, I almost said drily. But I have some sense.

I hung up the receiver and snuggled back under the covers. It was a cool foggy October morning. I should be up and about. I had a lot to do. And I was going to talk to John Solomon. If he were in town. Lord, I hoped so. John Solomon looks like an overstuffed lizard. His skin is yellowish and unhealthy. His eyes are thick-lidded, giving him a Mongolian aspect. He moves slowly, heavily, giving unconscious sighs as he struggles up from behind his desk. He is the best private investigator on the Coast. He handles all kinds of investigations, searches for missing spouses and snatched kids, industrial espionage, divorce work, office surveillance. He costs a fortune but he is quick, accurate, and makes a clam look outgoing.

I reached over and flicked on the coffeemaker and watched the amber liquid drip into the pot. When it was ready, I poured a cup and cradled it between my hands. I loved Saturday mornings, staying in bed an extra moment, drinking coffee and lazily planning my day. I worked, of course. The office was open from ten to two to give my working-class clients a chance for appointments. Most of them have the kind of jobs where you don't ask to take care of personal problems during working hours. Even so, Saturdays were slower paced, no court appearances, no calls from other lawyers.

But today the Saturday morning charm was absent. Greg's call and the continuing prick of worry over Francine Boutelle obtruded into my workaday schedule.

Greg. He was not an altogether comfortable person. Intense, energetic, quick-tempered, he was consumed with ambition. I sometimes had the feeling that his interest in me was the first time he had ever taken his eyes from his main goal: the aggrandizement of Gregory Garrison.

But was it an aberration?

That is one of the difficulties in being rich. And the primary reason, though not the only one, why the rich marry the rich. A man can't be after your money if he has potsful himself.

Greg. I could see him so clearly, his thick black hair and vividly blue eyes. He had the kind of looks political candidates need these days, a handsome face, a trim athletic build. This wasn't what attracted me. His appeal was a sense of leashed power, of intense energy, and vitality. He radiated excitement, like a superb horse waiting for the starting gun.

He was, in essence, a very attractive animal.

Our minds are interesting creatures with their incredible ability to sort and store infinite amounts of information, to catalogue experience and retrieve it.

That was what my mother said, some years earlier, about Toby.

"Quite an attractive animal, isn't he?" she asked sarcastically.

Toby, with his marvelous capacity for avoiding the unpleasant, had just left our tiny apartment. I stood stiffly in the center of the little living room, but I think I can fairly say that I wasn't defensive or even angry. I went straight to the point.

"Why are you here, Grace?"

"Margaret Fitzgerald called me yesterday. She said she couldn't believe it, she really couldn't—"

I almost smiled.

"—but the daughter of a friend of hers had told her mother that you were . . . sharing an apartment with a man!"

And I was. I was a first-year law student as was Toby. We had met that summer at Lake Tahoe and it seemed a fun idea. I hadn't, of course, broadcast it. Whose damned business was it, anyway?

"As I wrote you and Dad, I am sharing an apartment with another law student."

"That wasn't quite honest, was it?"

"It was quite honest. His name is Toby Weston. He's from Spokane, Wash."

"For heaven's sake, K.C., if you want . . . why don't you marry him?"

"I have absolutely no interest in marrying Toby."

At her look of total dismay, I took a little pity.

"Look, Grace," I said gently, "*Autre temps, autre moeurs.* Life is different." I looked around the boxy room with its array of ferns and plants

(Toby liked growing things) and the worn Persian rug and stacks of books. "This is just a temporary thing. We'll go to school and we'll be friends and have a lot of fun and one day it will all be over."

I had seen how it would go. And it had. Toby, ebullient, entertaining and macho, split the pots and pans with me, upon graduation, and loaded up the rental hitch for the drive back to Spokane.

"Look me up, K.C., if you ever come up my way."

"I will, Toby. Take care of yourself."

"Right. You, too."

But this camaraderie, and, admit it, friendly sex, was absolutely foreign to Grace.

She had stood in that dingy little apartment that day and summed me up as a trollop.

"But if you aren't even in love with him . . ." she began heatedly.

"Grace, let's drop it," and my voice began to have an edge.

She had stared at me for a long moment. It must have been hard for her. She couldn't threaten to disinherit me. The chips jumped generations according to old K.C. III's will. I had the income from the trust upon reaching the age of 21 and I could, if I wished, live with a dozen guys and no one could cut off my cash.

Grace drew her breath in sharply. "I don't know what your father will think."

I knew. I had told Dad, in a gentle way, before I had left for school. He had tamped his pipe and looked out the window of his chambers and said quietly, "Sometimes, K.C., a casual involvement can be quite . . . affecting."

I had patted his arm. "It will be all right."

He had nodded. "Just be careful of yourself, K.C."

I wasn't going to tell Grace about that talk. That would be a gratuitous insult. Instead, I just shrugged.

Her face flushed. "Perhaps we can buy you a stud farm," and she whirled on her spike heels and flung open the door.

I had never forgotten that moment. Angry? Some. But, mostly, that taunt hung in the back of my mind until an odd moment like this when the memory popped up so clearly and vividly I could once again smell the moist greenery of that tiny room and hear the sharp click of Grace's heels.

A stud farm. It must have hurt more than I had ever admitted.

I took another sip of coffee and made a face. It was cold. Irritably, I flung back the covers. My lovely Saturday morning wasn't fun anymore. I didn't even try to follow my usual routine. Instead, I dressed quickly, grabbed up my briefcase, and slammed out of the apartment.

I parked in my usual lot, a weed-pocked asphalt patch behind a bail-bond company. I paid a princely $15 a month for my slot. John Solomon's office was only a block from mine. His office didn't even have a storefront. It was tucked behind the Acme Cleaning Plant. A rickety outside stairway led up to a garage apartment that John had converted into offices.

I rang the bell and heard the sharp buzz. Nothing happened. I rattled the screen door, tried the knob. The door was locked. On a weekday, you could go right in and Mitzi, fat and fiftyish, would wave you to a seat in a ratty rattan chair while she yelled over her shoulder, "Hey, Solly, you got a lady."

I jabbed the bell again.

"Coming. Coming." The door swung slowly in and John looked sleepily out. For the first time, it occurred to me that the apartment might be both office and home.

"I'm sorry if I woke you, John."

He shook his big head slowly. "No matter." He cleared his throat. "It *is* Saturday."

"I need help."

He sighed, opened the door wider for me then led the way into his office. He squeezed behind his desk and flicked on a gooseneck lamp.

"What's happened, a murder?"

"Nothing that easy."

His watery brown eyes looked at me curiously. I took a deep breath and told him about Francine Boutelle's approach, her accusations about my Dad and her claims that she had something on all of us, including Grace.

"So," I concluded, "I want everything you can scrape out from under a rock about Francine Boutelle, everything, where she came from, where she's worked, her boyfriends, what she likes to drink, every damn thing you can come up with."

"It will cost a lot of money," he warned.

"Money I've got."

He nodded. "Okay, K.C. I'll put Pamela on it."

Pamela Reeves is John's high-class operative. She has a B.A. in elementary education which, she discovered, pays on a level with clerking at the five and dime. She discovered, too, that she has a talent for getting people talking and finds everybody fascinating. She is superb at joining an office staff and finding out who's filching the company blind.

"I need as much as you can get to me by Monday noon."

"Jesus," he sighed.

"I'm a good customer."

John sighed again. "I was going to go to the lake with my daughter."

"I didn't know you had a daughter."

"She doesn't know she has a father, I work so hard."

I grinned. "Sad."

Slowly, he smiled, too. "I would only do this for a beautiful blonde with velvety brown eyes."

"And money," I added drily.

"Well, that too."

We left it that I would pick up whatever he had managed to discover at noon on Monday. As I left, he was dialing the phone. John might look sleepy but I would get a bulging folder full of facts.

My office was packed with waiting clients. I didn't give the Carlisles another thought until the phone rang at three. I excused myself from the worried couple whose tax return had been plucked for an audit and answered it.

"K.C.?"

"Yes," and I just managed not to sound impatient. After all, Priscilla couldn't know how busy I was.

"I have to talk to you."

Priscilla's voice is as soft and breathy as the sex symbol in a Swedish film. I find it exceedingly irritating.

"I'm busy," I said sharply. "I have clients in my office."

She ignored that. After all, what did my clients matter to her? "Can you come over now?" she demanded.

"No."

"K.C., this is important!"

I glanced at my watch. Three-fifteen. I had one more client in the waiting room. "I'll drop by around five."

It was a quarter to five when I found a parking slot a few doors down from Priscilla's condominium in Gloucester Square. The row of narrow-fronted, Jamestown-style attached houses were beautifully designed, expensively executed, and ludicrously out of place in La Luz.

Priscilla opened the door herself. She led the way to a sunken living room with a fluffy white shag carpet and chocolate-colored wingback chairs on either side of a Delft tile fireplace.

I sank gratefully into one of the huge chairs. Priscilla walked on to the bar. "What will you have?"

"Does the house run to Margaritas?"

"Sure."

It was excellent, the glass chilled and the rim salted. I took a slow satisfying taste. I do love Margaritas. I felt the tension of the day drain away—until I looked at Priscilla in the chair opposite.

Priscilla and I are both blondes, but that, I hope, is where the resemblance ends. Her eyes are the empty china blue of a 1910 doll and her complexion the peaches and cream of a 1925 Gibson girl. Usually. Today, she stared at me, her face greyish, her eyes strained. She huddled in her chair, clutching a tumbler with three inches of neat Scotch.

"For Pete's sake, Prissy, what's wrong?"

She took a hefty swallow of her drink. "Nothing's really wrong," she said unconvincingly, "I just wanted to talk to you."

Priscilla paints china plates. I play racquetball. Her idea of fun is Las Vegas. Dick and Jane and Spot were likely the leading characters in the last book she ever read. She and I have more in common than I and an *ayatollah*—but not a lot.

I just looked at her.

She fidgeted, took another big swallow—there was nothing weak about Priscilla's liquor consumption, apparently—and blurted out, "How are you going to vote on the trust?"

I continued to look at her. If she had asked for the latest quote on the stock market, I could not have been more surprised.

She mistook my shock for obstruction.

"K.C.," and her husky voice was almost inaudible, "please, you can't do it to me, you can't. You always said, a long time ago, if I ever needed anything, you would help. Please, you have to vote for it."

"Wait a minute, Prissy," I said soothingly. "Slow down. I haven't said I wasn't going to vote for it. But let me be sure I understand. You want me to vote to dissolve the trust?"

She beamed. "Yes, oh yes, K.C."

"Why?"

The happy smile at my understanding dissolved like a cube of sugar in boiling coffee.

"Why?" she parried.

"Why do you want the trust dissolved?"

"For the money."

"Yes, Priscilla," I said patiently, "I understand that. There will be a lot of money if the trust is dissolved. Why do you need that kind of money?"

"Well, it . . . I mean, after all, K.C., think what we can do with that kind of money. Furs and jewels and . . . I think I'll go to Paris, that's what I think I will do."

Paris is a damn long way from Las Vegas, but there would always be Monaco.

I stared speculatively at Prissy, at her glistening white blond hair and soft body and strained face.

"I might vote to dissolve," I said slowly, spacing it out, "if . . ."

"If what?"

"If you'll tell me the truth. About why you want the money."

She finished her drink and avoided my eyes. "Oh, it's just that I'd like to be free, and the money, that much money, well, everything would be all right. If I can just get the money."

I didn't say a word. I waited until, reluctantly, warily, she looked in my eyes.

"How much does Francine want, Prissy?" I asked quietly.

Her hands flew to her throat, an interesting example of primeval instinct. She stared at me, her eyes wide and frightened. She tried to speak and couldn't.

"Fifty thousand?" I asked.

She huddled deeper in her chair, a bird waiting for the cat to pounce.

"Come on, Prissy," I said tiredly. "Tell me."

She shook her head, back and forth, back and forth.

"It can't be that awful," I encouraged gently. After all, Priscilla had just turned 25 and she had not, despite her fondness for Las Vegas, been exposed to much vice. Whatever secret she hid must be magnified in her own mind. In the 1980s, it would take a truly horrendous deed to excite much public interest. Prissy was just a kid, a voluptuous and stupid kid.

"Don't be frightened, Priscilla." I spoke as if to a small child. "The Boutelle woman is out after all of us. She tried to get fifty thousand from me, saying she could prove Dad took a bribe on the Levy case and you know that's ridiculous."

I could tell from Priscilla's lack of response that she had no idea what the Levy case was and, further, could not care less. It was that quality in Priscilla which made sustained sympathy a little difficult. Still, she looked so much like a terrified and cornered animal that I continued.

"Look, Priscilla, I'll help you. But you are going to have to tell me what's wrong."

She licked her lips. "The trust. If you will vote to dissolve the trust . . ."

I interrupted sharply. "Not until you tell me what you are afraid of."

She pushed up from her chair and crossed to the bar. She poured her glass full of Scotch and took another drink.

Even for a drinker, she was having a bit too much. I had never thought of Priscilla as a drinker. But really, I had seen little of Priscilla these last years. What did I know about her? For all I knew, she might souse her way through every day.

She turned around but stayed at the bar, leaning against it.

"If I tell you, then will you promise to vote to dissolve the trust?"

Priscilla was right on one count. It didn't matter a damn to me whether the trust ended or continued. But I had enough experience to know that great sums of money change life. Whether you wish it or not. The Mercedes salesmen would come. Brokers would call. Slick, hungry-eyed predators would always be near, waiting their chance.

But I was a big girl.

It would be a challenge, too, to make something useful and satisfying of life even though you knew that whatever you wanted, if it were for sale, could be bought.

"K.C.," and the appeal in her voice was unmasked, "please help me. I have to have the money. I have to."

It was the most direct real emotion I had ever heard from Priscilla.

I almost said yes without another word because it was so painful to see, like a fluffy plastic doll suddenly come to life. But I knew I would never again come so close to discovering what lay behind her distress.

I tried a different tack.

"Is it a man, Priscilla?"

I hated to think of unleashing Priscilla with several million dollars. I could imagine how she would be ripped off, monetarily and emotionally.

She stared at me for a long moment. Behind her china blue eyes, she was thinking furiously. Abruptly, she nodded.

"That's it, K.C. Oh, I didn't want anyone ever to know and that awful Miss Boutelle, she threatened to put it all in that magazine and then I would lose him."

"Threatened to put what?"

"All about me and him."

I gave a little shrug. "I can't see breaking the trust on that account, Priscilla. I mean, for God's sake, nobody cares who you are sleeping with. Certainly it's not worth fifty thousand to hide."

Panic flared in her face again. "You don't understand. He's married. His wife is an invalid. And besides," she said triumphantly, "he's Catholic."

I suppose I must have underestimated Priscilla. She had obviously been reading Ann Landers all these years.

"Hmm, that's a problem," I agreed. Of course, it was possible, with Priscilla's mind and body, that she might fall for the oldest line of all, but, somehow, circa 1980, I didn't think so.

"Who is he?"

She stared down at the fluffy white carpet, then said abruptly, "Hamilton Fisher," then looked up to see how I reacted.

I've been in enough trials where the witnesses shock and surprise you, to learn not to change expression. So Priscilla didn't get any reaction from me.

I knew Ham Fisher, of course. Big, rawboned, and cheerful, he had the Cadillac franchise. He also had an invalid wife. But Priscilla couldn't know that I knew even more about Ham Fisher. I knew that for years he had quietly taken out to dinner, when he was in Los Angeles, a sorority sister of mine who was a film editor at Columbia.

It was a brilliant piece of improvisation on Priscilla's part. And it showed how far she was willing to go to hide whatever dreadful specter Francine Boutelle threatened to expose. Of course, it didn't show too much concern for Ham Fisher.

Priscilla crossed the room and leaned down to clutch my arm. "Please, K.C." Her soft whisky-laden breath engulfed me. "Please vote yes. If you don't—oh, it could ruin my life."

She was lying about Ham Fisher. Lying, too, I thought, that her secret concerned a man. But there was something there, something that terrified Priscilla. The hand on my hand was damp with sweat.

I hesitated for another moment. After all, if I could wring the truth out of her, maybe there would be some way for me to quell Boutelle. But maybe not.

Maybe Priscilla's secret was truly appalling.

"All right," I said abruptly. I couldn't bear to hear her beg. It wouldn't hurt me to vote to dissolve although I might be doing Prissy a disservice in the long run, opening her up to more grief by making her vulnerable to the greedy and unprincipled people who cluster near great wealth. But I had decided. "All right, Prissy, I'll vote yes. But look at me."

She stared down at me with wide and fuzzy blue eyes.

"Why don't you let me handle this thing with Boutelle? If you'll tell me all the details, exactly what she plans to publish, maybe I can head her off."

She was tempted. For a moment, she wavered, then, wearily, hopelessly, she shook her head. "No. There's nothing anyone can do. Nothing."

There was stark despair in her voice.

FOUR

Travis's call came Sunday afternoon.

It was typical that it was person-to-person, not direct dialed. Travis had never been careful about pennies. Not about dollars, either.

"K.C., it's swell to hear your voice."

"It's nice to hear yours, Travis."

After that insincere exchange, he got down to business.

"I wanted to have a word with you. Have you talked to Edmond?"

"Not since last Christmas," I said drily. "Have you?"

"No, I haven't, as a matter of fact. Thing about it is, I have a little note here from Kenneth about a meeting to dissolve the trust."

"I received one, too."

"Good-oh." Travis had spent a year in Australia during his college days. He had come home with several Aussie expressions and a full red beard which was just now becoming fashionable. "Well, no point in talking to Edmond. You know how he is, the long view instead of the short. But I've got my heart set on a rather special artifact, K.C. It's a private sale, a once-in-a-lifetime chance." He paused, said dramatically. "A Ming vase, absolutely beautiful. I didn't think there was any way I could manage it. I don't want to be specific but prices in the art world have gone 'round the bend, right 'round the bend. If we dissolve the trust, I can do it. Hell, if we dissolve the trust . . ." I suppose his mind was so flooded with the glories of what he could buy that he was rendered speechless for a moment. Then, in a rush, "So the thing is, old top, I wondered if you could see your way clear to voting to dissolve. I mean, there must be some things you'd like to do if you had some extra money, a condo in Aspen, maybe, or a little cottage in Carmel?"

Travis might not be a soulmate of a brother but he had remembered, obviously, how much I liked to ski and my fondness for that little jewel of a seaside city. To have put that much effort into thinking of the other guy indicated an overwhelming need on his part to be persuasive.

I decided not to prolong the suspense. "I'm voting to dissolve, Travis."

I heard his sigh of relief, all the way from Chicago. That was as revealing in its way as the entire conversation.

"Excellent," he boomed. "Absolutely excellent. Hold to it, K.C. I'll see you tomorrow."

I had intended to tell him we would all be dining at Mother's, but, his objective secured, he was off the phone.

I almost laughed, but, somehow, none of it was funny.

I half expected Edmond to call. He was an astute businessman. One secret of astuteness is never to go into a meeting until you have your ducks lined up. So, it wasn't a surprise when Pat told me Edmond was on the line Monday morning. I had to file a brief by noon and I was still working on the last few pages, but I took the call.

"K.C.?"

"Yes, Edmond."

"I wondered if you might be free for lunch. At the Atheneum Club."

"I'm sorry, Edmond, I can't make it today. I have another engagement. But would another day do?"

He paused. "Actually, K.C., I had hoped to talk to you before we attend the meeting scheduled at Kenneth's office this afternoon."

"Oh?" I replied noncommittally. I saw no reason to make it easy for Edmond.

"Yes." He paused again and I could picture him, mouth pursed, eyebrows drawn in a dark frown. "It is difficult to explain financial matters adequately over the telephone, but I am hoping to gain your agreement, K.C. Normally, I would oppose dissolution of the trust. After all, the taxes . . ."he took a deep breath, ". . . the taxes on my portion of the undistributed income will, as you appreciate, be devastating. For this reason, I would be much more prudent to vote against dissolution but, the fact of the matter is, I have an opportunity of a kind that could result in tremendous profitability. You will understand if I am somewhat vague about the matter. I do, after all, have to protect my fellow investors, but it is an opportunity to join in a drilling venture in the Gulf that has high prospects of success."

"I see. In that event, Edmond, I imagine you will be pleased to know that I do intend to vote to dissolve the trust."

He managed to disguise better than Travis his quick intake of breath but his tone told me so much more than he intended.

"Good. That will be . . . very helpful to me. I appreciate your frankness, K.C. I will see you this afternoon, then."

If there had been a fabulous investment opportunity awaiting him, he would have been happy at my agreement, but his voice was tired and strained. He didn't want to dissolve the trust, but, for some dark and urgent reason, it was imperative to Edmond that he have access to a very great deal of money.

I stared at the phone for a long moment after he hung up. I had, earlier in the morning, considered sending Pat to pick up the report on Francine Boutelle. I would take a look at it, snatch a few minutes after the meeting at Kenneth's and before the dinner at Mother's. I changed my mind. I yanked my legal pad to me and began swiftly one word, one sentence, one paragraph after another, to finish the brief for Amundsen vs. The City of La Luz. It would be good enough, had to be good enough. It was, abruptly, very important to me to find out now, as soon as possible, every last thing I could about Francine Boutelle. I didn't like the way she was leaning on the Carlisles. I didn't like what was happening to Priscilla and Travis and Edmond. And me.

Priscilla was scared silly. Travis, foolish, foppish, good-natured Travis, was desperately worried. Edmond was a cornered man. And I had my own fears.

I met Pamela Reeves in a back booth at the Blue Grotto. As the cocktail waitress brought our Margaritas, Pamela handed me a yellow file folder and sat back with a tired sigh.

"If you weren't such a good customer, I wouldn't have managed it. I'm going to go home now and sleep for three days."

I scanned the dossier.

> BOUTELLE, FRANCINE EMILY. B. Feb. 3, 1954, Venice, Ca. Parents, John Edward and Katharine Celeste Boutelle. Parents divorced (date as yet not obtained). Reared by mother who worked in a VandeKamp's Bakery. Graduated Venice High School, June 18, 1971. Waitress at Forsby's in Hollywood, 1972–75. Graduated UCLA, BA in journalism, 1975. Aspiring starlet. Francine worked on a Long Beach paper for three years, joined an LA paper in 1978. In February of 1980, she started to work as a cocktail waitress at the Cocoa Butter in downtown LA.

"That's odd," I murmured. "Hey, Pamela, why the switch from a newspaper to a cocktail joint?"

"I don't know yet. I'm still trying to find out."

"She told me she was working for *Inside Out.* What's the deal?"

"She is, sort of. I called *Inside Out,* pretended I was looking for a job. They didn't have any openings. Then I asked about my old friend, Francine Boutelle. This editor was a little snippy about it, said Boutelle was doing an article on assignment but she was not a regular staff member."

So Boutelle was using the Carlisles to get started with *Inside Out.*

"How about men?"

Pamela shrugged. "Here in La Luz or earlier?"

"Both."

"There are only so many hours in the day."

"Start with La Luz."

"So far, that's all I've had a chance to really check out. She has a nosy neighbor, a Mrs. Collins. She allows that Francine has a beau, but she's never really seen him. Just glimpses of a dark topcoat and the sounds of a man talking."

"That's interesting," I said quickly. "Find out more, if you can. Francine's only been in town six weeks. Is it someone she's met in that time or did she know somebody here before she came?"

Pamela frowned. "It's tough, looking here, K.C. She doesn't have friends or co-workers I can get close to and pump."

"Do the best you can."

"I'm pretty sure of one thing, she's never been married and nobody mentions a particular man when I ask about her."

I frowned. "Maybe she's a lesbian."

Pamela looked at me thoughtfully. "Maybe, but I don't think so. I spent five hours with her in the bar at Nightingale's Saturday night and I never got a hint of anything like that."

I tapped the dossier. "Is that how you found out most of this?"

"Mostly from talking to her."

"Five hours?" I repeated.

Pamela smiled wryly. "She likes to drink. I thought maybe I could really get her started the way she was lapping up the Scotch, but I would guess she's been drinking a lot for a long time. She talked, yeah, but there was nothing maudlin, nothing to really give her away."

I looked down at the folder. I had her birth date and where she had gone to school. Swell. I needed more than that. A lot more.

"How do you size her up?"

The answer came back like a ball off the wall. "Smart. Tough. Absolutely ruthless."

That was my appraisal, too. Unfortunately.

"No chinks?"

"None apparent." Pamela frowned. "I don't know, though I think . . ." She paused, rubbed the rim of her glass. "I don't know for sure, K.C., I can't swear to it, but I think she's really hot for some guy. This was toward the end. Lord, it must have been almost two in the morning. It was the last gig. You know. Nightingale's runs to jazz combos with female blues singers. This was a really good one and she spent a lot of time with 'My Man' and 'Summertime', stuff like that. Francine got started on a kind of diatribe about being poor and making it all by yourself without anybody to give a bloody damn and how you have to be tough to do it. I kind of faded out, I mean, I've heard the working girl makes good story before, and by the time I tuned back in, the tenor of it had changed. She was intense, really soft-throated and husky, saying it could be fantastic if the right two people got together, that they could make anything happen, anything. I don't know whether she was thinking about what she wanted to have happen or whether she had already teamed up with Mr. Fantastic. I was a little fuddled at that point. Believe me, I didn't sit around in bars drinking double Scotches until I took up this PI business. Whether she was dreaming or glorying, I just don't know. At the very start of the evening, I bumped her elbow, you know, spilled her drink, and offered to buy her another. That's one way to get to talking to someone at a bar. Anyway, it worked and we commiserated about being two working girls out in the big city with nobody to buy our drinks. You have to understand that this was all spread out over several hours. We did have some gents join us at one time or another, but, and this seems significant to me, she wasn't really on the prowl for some guy to take her home. At the same time, like I told you, there wasn't any hint that she was interested in me. So, it makes you think. Maybe she's some important guy's girl friend and he had to be home with the momma-hubby on Saturday night. Anyway, for what it's worth, I think she's really into something with somebody."

It did interest me. Sex, money, and pride rule the world.

"Okay, Pamela. Find him."

Pamela clutched her head. "My big mouth. What about my three days' sleep?"

"Some other week," I replied unfeelingly. "Keep after it for me, Pamela." I studied Francine's job list. "Find out why she ended up in a club again."

Pamela finished her Margarita. "It will cost a lot."

"I don't care what it costs."

Pamela looked at me curiously, but she didn't say anything. It was pretty obvious that this wasn't just another job to me.

It wasn't. Not by a long shot. I could tell Grace and Priscilla not to worry, just to tell me all about it and let me handle it because I couldn't imagine that either of them would have anything really serious to fear from Boutelle's revelations, no matter how unpleasant. I didn't feel that way about my own secret. I couldn't bear to have everyone know about Sheila and me. I couldn't bear it.

But how, I agonized, could Francine Boutelle know what really happened to Sheila? Only Sheila and I were there. Only the two of us.

I bought Pamela the best lunch in the house. Usually, I love to eat at the Blue Grotto but I wasn't hungry and I glanced again and again at the typed report as if I might find something there, anything, that would give me some leverage on Francine Boutelle.

Back in my office, I tried to concentrate on my work, and I did finish a new will for the Frankfurts and the adoption papers on the Morrison baby, but it was automatic, only the surface of my mind engaged.

I was really thinking about Francine Boutelle and her manuscript. Was it a blind? Was she really writing on the Carlisles or was that just a clever way of phrasing a blackmail demand? Putting some teeth in her request?

I doodled on a legal pad, a five followed by a line of fat round zeroes.

No, the manuscript must be real. She was freelancing it to *Inside Out,* so she must intend to come up with a story. How would she handle it? Would she delete the spicy bits for those who paid? It would be something like that. Even if everyone anted up, she would still owe the magazine a story. That wouldn't be hard to write, however. There was certainly plenty to say about the Carlisles, even without the more lurid passages on everyone's personal lives. Wouldn't the managing editor wonder, though? *Inside Out* liked scandal, thrived on it. How could Francine explain an innocuous article? Of course, she could claim she hadn't found out anything really racy. The magazine was based in LA so the editor wouldn't have any local knowledge. She could still rag the family hard about its money and extravagances.

I didn't give a damn what she wrote about us in that vein, but I was going to keep her from opening up the hidden seams, if I could. And I wasn't going to see any of us pay her a penny.

Wasn't I? Just how did I think I could prevent it?

I could threaten her with libel suits. But that was revenge, not prevention, and likely would come to little anyway. Truth is still a defense in libel. Of course, she could be in trouble on the basis of malice if everyone testified that she had attempted blackmail. But would they? In any event, I didn't want recompense. I wanted to prevent publication.

By the time I arrived at Kenneth's office for the meeting of the Cochran-Carlisle beneficiaries, I had some ideas. Nothing foolproof, but a couple of them merited consideration.

Kenneth's receptionist couldn't quite disguise her curiosity. "Yes, Miss Carlisle, Mr. Carlisle is expecting you. Please go to the main conference room."

"And that is?" I asked gently.

"Oh, I thought you'd probably . . . that is, excuse me, it's the fourth door on the right. Everyone else is there."

I had realized I was running a little late. I wondered how much of it was my disinclination to come at all. I found the proper door and, as I opened it, I saw the receptionist craning her head to watch. It must be causing quite a bit of interest among the help, this gathering of the Carlisle clan.

The men rose as I stepped inside. This was my first visit to Kenneth's conference room and it was a sight truly to delight the heart of an Establishment lawyer. A massive mahogany table with inlaid copper panels offered seats for twelve. Heavy red velvet drapes framed the windows. The walls were paneled in oak. Real oak, not pressed plastic. It was ponderous, sumptuous, and probably quite soothing to corporate clients.

I nodded to the chorus of hellos and slipped into an empty chair. We hardy band of Carlisles did not, of course, nearly fill the twelve seats. We looked rather a small group in that proud room.

Kenneth sat at the head of the table. "Now that K.C. is here, we can get under way."

So I wasn't to be Katharine Cecilia. That showed, perhaps, the stress on Kenneth, that he had reverted to our childhood relationship.

It was the first time he had called me K.C. since our quarrel over my use of the initials in my professional listing.

He began to describe, in an incredibly boring fashion, the formation of the Carlisle fortune and the creation of the trust. Instead of listening, I looked at old K.C.'s descendants.

Edmond sat to Kenneth's right. Edmond is fair, with thinning blond hair. His pale complexion emphasizes the lines that bracket his eyes and mouth. He stared down at a legal pad, his mouth a grim straight line.

Priscilla sat to Kenneth's left. She wore a mauve suede jacket and her hair looked like waves of honey. She was absolutely stunning. Until, I thought unkindly, she spoke. She turned just then and looked down the table toward me and once again the appeal in her eyes was so strong that it shocked me.

I gave a tiny, almost indiscernible nod and her whole body relaxed.

Travis saw it, of course. Travis is the kind of man who never misses a nuance. His lively malicious green eyes looked at me inquiringly. I smiled blandly and turned my face toward Kenneth, cupping my chin in my hands and feigning fascination in the recital of facts and figures. Mostly figures. My God, we were rich. Or were going to be after the vote.

Kenneth paused. He stared down at the thick sheaf of papers. He has a classically handsome face, broad and sturdy with a bold nose and dark blue eyes. His hair is blond, like most of the Carlisles, but his is thick and curly, which makes him look younger than he is. He didn't look especially young today, the skin beside his mouth pinched and white. Abruptly, he closed the folder and looked around the table.

"So that's it. I have, as I explained, divided the shares of stock in the various companies absolutely equally. Each beneficiary will receive precisely the same amount. I have, in addition, worked out the most feasible tax plan. The upshot of it is, each of us will come out with about three and a quarter million."

It was very quiet. No one spoke or moved.

Kenneth looked at Priscilla. "Do I have a motion to dissolve?"

Priscilla nodded and I remembered that, presumably, it was she who had engineered this meeting.

"I move that the Cochran-Carlisle Trust be dissolved in accordance with the proposals Kenneth has made." She said it by rote.

Travis seconded the motion almost before she finished speaking.

The ayes went around the table and then it was my turn. I looked at them, my brothers and cousins, at their guarded faces and worried eyes, and I wanted to cry out, "Wait a minute, why are we doing this? Why are we letting a cheap little bitch off the LA streets lean on us? We're Carlisles, we can handle her. If we don't want this vote, if it's wrong and foolish, let's fight."

But the vote was already stacked. I knew that. I knew, too, that if I broke it out into the open, I would be standing naked by myself. Those closed desperate faces told me that.

Did I want to talk about Sheila? Would I ever be willing to talk about Sheila?

So, after a long pause, a pause during which they all turned to look at me, as if I were some curious, perhaps threatening, stranger, I said, "Aye," and the voting went on.

It came out 5–0 and we were instant millionaires.

I didn't hear a single cheer.

FIVE

Amanda opened the front door at Mother's.

"Miss K.C., oh, honey, it's so good to see you. It's been so long," and she beamed at me.

I reached out and took her work-worn hands. "Mandy, you look so pretty."

If possible, her smile widened. For an instant, a wonderful timeless instant, we stood there, loving each other, secure in an insecure world.

I did love Amanda. And I knew that she loved me. Her love had made my childhood bearable. Oh, my father cared, in his distant and aloof fashion. He had, as I grew older, admired me, seen in my mind his own incisive intellect. But Sheila was my mother's favorite. Always. Even after she died. It was then that Amanda salvaged me, saved me from the grey and icy limbo that my life became.

"I want you to come into town," I said abruptly, "next week. We will have lunch. And visit. You can tell me all about Rudolph and his family."

Rudolph was Amanda's son and she was so proud of him. Rightly so. With Dad's help, he had gone to college and then to medical school and he was now a general practitioner in La Luz.

Amanda had grown up when blacks rode the backs of buses, when most colleges were barred to them. To have a son who had not only finished college but become a doctor . . . her life was complete. She said that to me one day, so simply and directly. I had scolded her a little. "Don't be silly, Amanda. You are going to live to be an old, old lady. Until I'm an old lady, too, and I shall come to visit you and we will talk about the impossible world and all the changes we've seen, as old ladies do."

She had smiled, but a little uncertainly. True, she loved me, but she didn't always understand me. "Miss K.C., you do talk nonsense, don't you?"

Now she stood in Mother's foyer, holding my hands, smiling at me. Her grey uniform was spotless as always, but she was beginning to look old, her once-wiry black hair almost totally white, her plump face thinned, her shoulders bowed.

I frowned. Amanda was too old for this kind of evening. My God, all of us were coming. That meant dinner for . . . I counted them up in my mind . . . dinner for nine. I heard the chatter of voices, light and deep, and the chink of glasses from the drawing room. Mother, of course, still had a drawing room.

"Amanda, who's helping you tonight?"

She looked a little surprised. "Jason. He's going to wait table."

Jason was her cousin and almost as old as she.

Dinner for nine and all the cooking and cleaning up that would entail.

"I'll bet you've been working since early this morning."

For just an instant, her shoulders sagged, then she said quickly, "It's all right, Miss K.C. And it's so nice to have everyone home again, even if it's only for a little while."

I slipped off my coat and she reached out to take it.

"I thought Dad set up an annuity for you, Mandy. You always said you were going to retire to a cabin out at the lake and spend the mornings fishing and the afternoons rocking on your front porch."

"Oh now, Miss K.C.," she chided, "you know your momma can't find anybody to take my place. Nobody wants to live in anymore. I'll take care of her for as long as I can because your poppa did everything for me. He put my Rudolph through school. If it wasn't for your poppa, Rudolph wouldn't be a doctor today."

Maybe not, but was Amanda supposed to pay for that for the rest of her life? And I wasn't surprised that Grace couldn't find anyone to take Amanda's place. Who wanted to work from dawn to dusk with only Thursday afternoons and Sundays off? The market for exploited servants is slim these days.

Grace was taking advantage of Amanda. Amanda knew it, too, but she was busy satisfying a debt that didn't exist. Dad wouldn't have expected Amanda to work forever just because he helped Rudolph. And, God knew, helping Rudolph was little enough to do for the sturdy little woman who kept our home running for all those years.

"Miss K.C.!"

"Yes."

"You don't say nothin' now to your momma. She has problems of her own. I tell you, Miss, she is all upset about something."

"That is no reason for you . . ."

"You hush now." Amanda looked at me sternly. "You are too young, Miss K.C. You see everything as so simple. Sometimes, it isn't so simple. Old Amanda knows what she has to do. You don't need to fret."

She looked so much like a little dark cat with fluffed fur that I grinned in spite of my resolve. Amanda was right. I did have a tendency to want to run everything, which isn't an altogether attractive trait. One I had picked up from Grace, perhaps?

I leaned down, hugged Amanda again and felt her body relax. "Don't worry, you old workaholic, I'll mind my own business."

But, as I walked down the central hallway toward the drawing room, I couldn't help judging the amount of work it took to keep this place going. Amanda used to have two full-time girls to do the cleaning. Did she still? I would check on that. Whatever Mother's problems, they didn't include money. She could certainly afford help for Amanda and I intended to make sure Amanda received it.

The house is a relic, a huge, energy-wasting, magnificent survivor of the time when every oil baron built for posterity. It is, as suits Northern California, a Spanish hacienda with immense cool dark rooms, a fountain in the central hallway and wide stone stairs leading up to the second and third floors. Fourteen bedrooms and a ballroom complete the upper stories.

The centerpiece of the drawing room is a fireplace with tiles from Taxco and a redwood mantel. Above the mantel hangs a Goya.

I paused in the wide doorway. Little clusters of my kin dotted the room.

Kenneth and Megan stood near the fireplace listening courteously to Travis. Travis's wife, Lorraine, watched, a skeptical expression on her face. Lorraine and Travis were, in my view, an odd combination, Travis exuberant, his face a little flushed now from his cocktail, and Lorraine withdrawn and aloof. She is an oncologist. She wore a grey chiffon dress and she looked impatient and bored.

Edmond and Sue sat stiffly on a Chippendale sofa, not looking convivial at all.

Mother was chatting with Priscilla but she saw me in the doorway.

"K.C., we've been waiting," she said immediately.

"Sorry. Hello, everyone."

"We'll go in to dinner now," and Mother nodded to Edmond to walk with her.

The dining room, with its heavy baroque furniture, depressed me as it always had, but, as usual at Mother's house, the dinner, thanks to Amanda, was superb.

The courses came and went, Jason serving from a sideboard and conversation surged up and down the table. It was quite animated for this particular group. It might almost be Christmas with its automatic cheer. The wineglasses sparkled and Jason kept them full. California wines, of course. There are no better in the world, despite what the French might think. It was a gay and voluble group with no outward sign of trouble—except for Edmond's somber face when the conversation lulled and the haunted look in Kenneth's eyes and Priscilla's strained stare.

I made polite conversation with Travis but it was Kenneth who dominated my thoughts. That look in his eyes reminded me of when he and Priscilla came to live with us. Edmond and Travis were already grown, Edmond married and well started on his investment career, Travis was in college. Uncle Bobby and Aunt Margaret were flying home to La Luz from Scottsdale, Ariz., one snowy December. He had been warned not to take off, a huge storm was building in the Sierras. But no one ever told Uncle Bobby what to do. They didn't find the wreckage until the following April.

Kenneth and I became allies of a sort against the coldness of my mother and the sense we both carried that life continued under siege. I don't remember much of Priscilla then. She had fitted into the house, content with a newly decorated room, absorbed in playing with a doll's house built like a Victorian castle.

I never had the feeling Priscilla grieved for her parents.

It was the summer after Kenneth and Priscilla came to live with us that Kenneth and I made detailed and intricate plans to run away. We wanted to follow the harvests all the way to Central America.

We hadn't included Priscilla or Sheila, of course. They were just little kids.

That wasn't the reason I left out Sheila. I didn't tell Kenneth. Perhaps, then, I hadn't even admitted it to myself, but I was running away from Sheila and mother's absorption in her. I just told Kenneth that Sheila and Prissy were too little to go and Kenneth agreed.

Prissy wouldn't have been interested in our scheme. She was never interested in anything outside her own comfort.

But Sheila was interested. She always in that huge house knew everything. Perhaps that summer day she followed us up the stairs, as we crept so surreptitiously toward the third floor. She could have hidden behind the blue urn on the first-floor landing, skipped on silent feet after us up the second flight and the third. In the dim and shadowy reaches of the ballroom, she must have crouched behind the covered grand piano as we tied the rope, then stayed behind as we started back downstairs.

There wasn't any logic, of course, to our plan to scramble three flights down a scratchy hemp rope. The house was locked at night but we could have started our trek soon after breakfast, making a nocturnal escape unnecessary. It would have been hours before we were missed. Who knows if we ever would have climbed down the rope at all? It was the romance of escape that fascinated us, the desire to be free and gone mixed in our minds with visions of desert brigands fleeing castle walls by rope.

So we left the rope, tied insecurely to a narrow band of metal, and crept down to the second floor; then, tired of stealth, burst out onto the front lawn to climb the huge sycamore that shaded the drive.

We couldn't see the window where we had tied the rope. It was on the west side of the house.

I was midway up the sycamore when I saw Rafael, the yard man, waving his arms and running toward the side of the house. It was such an odd sight, so unexpected, that I hung there openmouthed. Rafael never ran. He always moved slowly. Amanda said he had molasses in his bones.

Then the high shriek came.

I knew.

I clung to the rough bole of the sycamore, pushed my face against the bark until it hurt, and tried not to hear the trailing cry and the heavy thud.

Kenneth slid down the tree first and began to run.

I came, too, of course, and hung on the outskirts of the gathering circle and saw my little sister lying among the thick stems of the irises, one leg bent awkwardly beneath her.

It was the irises, they said later, that saved her life, cushioning her impact. They said it was a miracle, to fall three stories and suffer only a broken leg.

After the ambulance carrying Sheila and Mother left, Kenneth and I huddled in the shade at the side of the house. It was almost evening when my father came looking for us. We didn't know then what had happened to Sheila. We didn't know if she was going to live. That was what we thought, all that long afternoon, that we had killed Sheila. When my father found us, he understood. He consoled us and said she was going to be all right, that she had only a broken leg.

My mother came upon us then, angry and vengeful.

"If your sister's leg doesn't heal, if she always walks with a limp, well, we will know who is to blame, won't we, K.C.?"

I stood there with a stolid look on my face.

My father interrupted sharply, "Grace, that's enough. The children are upset as it is. They didn't intend for anyone to be hurt. And think of this, both K.C. and Kenneth are bigger and heavier than Sheila. If either of them had tried to go down the rope, it would have torn loose much sooner and we might have lost them."

"If Sheila is crippled . . ." Mother began.

That was all that mattered to her. Just Sheila. She wouldn't have cared if it had been Kenneth or me.

"Sheila is not going to be crippled," my father said angrily. Then he turned to me and Kenneth. "It's all right, children. Everything is all right."

I remembered that afternoon with crystal clarity, the heavy stillness about the house as we waited and the look of dread and despair in Kenneth's eyes.

It was the same look he had tonight as we all sat around the damask-covered table, talking lightly and inconsequentially.

A desperate haunted look.

Megan was aware of it. I saw her glance at him several times, quick worried looks.

After my talk with Priscilla, when I promised to vote as she wished, I had decided that Kenneth had agreed to the meeting to help his sister.

I couldn't imagine that Kenneth had ever done anything Francine Boutelle could exploit. Now I wasn't sure.

Travis, of course, hadn't missed any of it, Kenneth's demeanor, Megan's worry. He said to me softly, "Hey, what's eating little Sir Lancelot?"

I was surprised at my twinge of irritation. But I just shrugged and said, "Who knows?"

I deliberately turned away from Travis and began to talk to Lorraine.

Lorraine complained for a while about the smog in LA, the insolence of stewardesses, and the probable contamination of shellfish off San Francisco. Then, I suppose in an attempt at some social grace, she asked, "Are you enjoying your practice?"

"Yes, I really am. Though, as with most lawyers, it's either feast or famine, and, right now, I have way too much to do."

Lorraine frowned, thinking, I suppose, that if I organized well, anything could be managed.

"Do you do criminal work?"

"Some. Not a lot. I take anything that walks through the door," and smiled.

Lorraine didn't smile in return. "I wouldn't do criminal work if I were a lawyer," she said sharply.

"Really. Why not?"

"The kind of people who commit crimes do not deserve lawyers."

God. What a lovely outlook on life and jurisprudence.

"Well," I observed quietly, "perhaps it's a good thing you aren't a lawyer. Every lawyer has to do some criminal work. The court appoints lawyers to defend indigents who can't afford counsel."

Lorraine stabbed a fork into a piece. "That's what's wrong with this country. The government makes everything easy for the shiftless. If people don't have the money for a lawyer, then I don't see why the rest of us should pay for it."

"Actually, you don't pay for it," I explained, "unless your city has a public defender's office. When a lawyer is appointed by the court, he doesn't receive any recompense. It's *pro bono* work."

Lorraine spread butter (fresh butter churned in the kitchen) on hot parker house rolls (baked by Amanda) then paused to sip wine before resuming her diatribe against the shiftless poor getting free legal service.

"Besides," she concluded, "The whole system's wrong."

"Really?"

"Half the time, the guilty are acquitted and, even when they go to jail, it's only for a little while, then they let them out to prey on society again."

I took a drink of my wine. Was there any point in trying to talk to someone like Lorraine? Then I put my glass down and tried.

"Look, Lorraine, people are acquitted when the prosecution fails to convince a jury the defendant is guilty. Twelve people listened to the evidence and didn't buy it. As for paroling prisoners, the hope is for rehabilitation. It's hard enough for a man or woman to come back from prison and keep out of trouble but the longer time they spend in prison, the more brutalized they are and the less likely they are to make it on the street without going back to crime. Society isn't well served by keeping people jailed for long terms."

"If they are convicted a second time," Lorraine said, her mouth thin, "they should be put away for life."

"For life? Even if it's a kid who's stolen a car? He should go to the pen for life?"

"Yes. I have no sympathy with lawbreakers. None."

"Apparently not." I wondered how she felt about patients with a recurrence. But I suppose she saw no correlation between social malignancies and physical ills.

"In fact," she said heatedly, "I believe this country could benefit from looking at Saudi Arabia."

"Oh?"

"Yes. Saudi Arabia has very little crime."

"Really?" I knew that, of course. I was baiting her but some temptations are hard to resist.

"Why, yes. They don't fool around over there. If a man is a thief, they chop off one of his hands. If he steals again, they chop off the other."

"Pretty effective," I murmured.

"Oh, it is, it is. They have almost no thievery over there."

Yes, Saudi Arabia is tough on lawbreakers. Adultery rates a whacked-off head. That's pretty final. Saudi justice probably discourages a lot of adultery and encourages extreme care on the part of both thieves and amorous dalliers.

Lorraine continued to extol enthusiastically the virtues of Saudi culture.

I pictured her in one of those head-to-toe *burkas.* It might muffle her mouth so I decided Saudi Arabia couldn't be all bad.

I also decided that I would find someone besides Lorraine to talk to after dinner.

Dessert was freestone peaches Mandy had frozen last summer. Defrosted and topped with ice cream and a raspberry sauce, it was a delicious Peach Melba. Conversation was beginning to be desultory.

Mother caught everyone's attention.

"Let's go to the library for coffee." Her chin lifted. "We will decide what to do about that dreadful Boutelle woman."

SIX

As chairs scraped and were replaced and everyone began to move toward the doorway, I saw Megan tug at Kenneth's sleeve. He bent his head to listen, then shrugged, his hands turning palm upward.

I thought I could read that little scenario and it made me sad. Megan was asking who the Boutelle woman was and Kenneth was saying he didn't know. I wondered what Kenneth was going to tell Megan if everyone admitted to seeing Francine except him? How long would it take Megan to put it all together? Not long. Megan was smart. She was like so many of her kind, bright, well educated, devoted to good works, and, in a quiet and tolerant way, totally convinced of her own superiority. She never thought about it. It was a given. The Megan Carlisles of this world live in a rarefied atmosphere, luxurious homes, servants, attentive children, civic involvement. All Megan lacked to complete the picture were children, handsome, gifted, and, of course, innately superior.

It suggested to me that Kenneth had been playing around. That surprised me. A lot. Not that I thought Kenneth too moral for extra-curricular sex. I thought him too devoted. In his cold fish life, it always seemed to me that he had shown a surprising passion for Megan. I remembered the Christmas that they met. It was a debutante ball and a typical one. The girls, all in white, which always amused me, danced the first dance with their fathers. I was there, unwillingly, because mother was chairman of the ball committee. My own coming-out had been several years earlier. I was terribly bored that evening and had danced with dozens of eligible young men, none of whom interested me. Perhaps because they were so eligible. In any event, Kenneth and

I ended up in a corner, trying, not too hard, to talk to each other. He was in his second year at law school and insufferably superior to a mere college senior. Then, abruptly, he caught my arm.

"That girl, the one over there by the fern. Who is she?"

I craned my neck. I happened to know because she was the younger sister of a girl my age. "That's Megan Phillips."

"I want to meet her," and he had my arm and was steering me across the room.

I introduced them and Kenneth danced away with her. I don't think she ever had a chance to know another man. I never saw such a determined courtship. They were married when Kenneth finished law school and I thought that surely theirs would be for ever after. To all appearances, it was. And Megan campaigned hard for Kenneth, even though fish fries and county fairs are not exactly her style.

Greg despised Megan. It was funny I should think of that, but I knew it was so. She represented everything he most detested: privilege, inherited wealth, and station.

Actually, Megan was quite likable. She had a gentle dry sense of humor quite at odds with her severe appearance. She was kindly even though it was often a *noblesse-oblige* response. She was crazy about Kenneth. You couldn't miss that. It was in the way she looked up when he came in a room, the way she smiled when she caught his eye, the way she would reach out and lightly touch his arm.

So the whole thing was damn depressing. I felt tired suddenly. Tired of all the Carlisles and their problems. I had never cared for Kenneth and now it looked like he was cheating on the woman who truly loved him—and whom I thought he adored.

It reminded me that you can never be sure of anything— or anyone.

I would have bet a lot on Kenneth and Megan's marriage.

I moved toward the back of the library and stood by the fireplace and looked moodily into the fire. It crackled and hissed, smelling comfortably of hickory. But I wasn't comfortable. I wanted to go home.

Did I?

My apartment would be chilly, no fire laid, no eggshell thin china cups holding superb coffee. Greg probably wouldn't call or come by. I hadn't, after all, given him much reason to.

"K.C., will you pour, please?"

Grace's voice, so perfectly civilized, so right, brought me back to the room. I turned and crossed to the coffee service and began to pour. Amanda brought in a platter of cookies.

As everyone settled into chairs or on couches. Mother began to talk.

And I thought, oh wow, this is going to tear it for Kenneth.

"... and I felt if we talked it over, among ourselves, we might come up with a solution. Kenneth, of course, can tell us what our rights are legally."

Coffee spilled over the brim of the cup, splashing onto the saucer Edmond held.

"Hold up, K.C."

"Sorry."

"Here, Miss K.C. I'll take that cup. Pour Mr. Edmond a fresh one." As Amanda took the sloshing saucer, she bent near to me and said softly, "Don't you pay her no never mind, Miss K.C. Your poppa he told me once, he said, 'Miss K.C. will be the best lawyer of all, Amanda, you wait and see.'"

"It doesn't matter." But I couldn't resist the bitter comment, "It's so damn typical."

Grace had called and asked me to come, even gone so far as to say I approached problems like my father, but when she needed legal advice, why, apparently only men counted as lawyers. Obviously, too, she hadn't talked to Kenneth earlier. He looked stricken, then he rallied, "Aunt Grace, I'd be glad to help, but I'm afraid I don't know what you are talking about."

Grace can be obtuse sometimes. She said impatiently, "Why, Kenneth, of course you know. It's that Boutelle woman and that awful article she is writing about all of us. She told me she had talked to you."

For an instant, Kenneth looked grim and angry. Then he cleared his throat. "Oh. Of course. That reporter woman. I didn't remember the name."

"But Kenneth . . ." Mother began.

"As a matter of fact," he interrupted hastily, "I talked to her very briefly. Very briefly. I declined to be interviewed. I could tell it was a scandal-mongering kind of thing and I told her I wasn't interested."

A child of three could have seen that Kenneth was lying. Megan was no child. Her narrow face looked suddenly pinched and old.

Grace continued to be dense. "But Kenneth, I thought . . ."

"I warned her that the Carlisle family would not tolerate a libelous article."

Grace brightened. "So we can force her not to print it?"

"No," I said quietly, taking pity on Kenneth. "There's no way, Grace. However, we can sue the socks off her if we don't like it."

"K.C.," Grace said sharply, "the point is, we don't want it printed."

"I understand what you want, Grace. The point is, there isn't a damned thing you can do to stop her."

"It's blackmail," Edmond said harshly.

Everyone looked at him.

"It's blackmail, that's all there is to it," he said again.

"We could buy the magazine," Sue suggested.

Edmond nodded. "It's going to come down to that."

"What good will that do?" Travis asked. "She can just sell the damned article somewhere else."

Edmond shook his head. "Oh no, we will use a dummy company to buy the magazine, then instruct the editor to buy the article. When it is in his possession, we will destroy it. She cannot legally sell it elsewhere."

I poured myself a cup of coffee and thought what a wonderful thing wealth is. Edmond was so confident of what money could buy, but I had known a few people in journalism. The editor of *Inside Out* was probably not the most likable guy in the world or he wouldn't work for such a destructive organ, but his hackles would flare at the idea of being bought off. One way or the other, the article would see print.

"Fat chance," I remarked.

They all looked at me.

"Sorry, friends, but I don't think it will work to buy the magazine.

Magazines aren't hunks of cheese. You would never succeed in telling an editor what to print."

"If we own it, we can control it."

"If the editor is like some I've known, he will listen to you, mumble something in reply, print the damn article, and quit."

"But we can. . . ."

I looked at Edmond with interest. "What can we do? Besides fire him and that will be too late."

"We have to do something," Priscilla said throatily.

"Pay up," I said briefly.

"But that's . . ." Edmond began.

"Blackmail," I agreed. "But what else can you do, if you really don't want her to write all these . . . interesting things about us?"

It was very quiet and no one exchanged glances.

"It's quite absurd," Lorraine said suddenly. She turned to Travis, "You haven't talked to this woman, have you?"

"No, I . . . uh . . . haven't had the pleasure. Just as soon not, considering the bother she's causing."

I recognized a particular tone in Travis' voice, one of insouciance and carelessness. It was just the way he would answer Mother on those long-ago mornings when she would inquire what time he had come in the night before. "Oh, early on, Mater, early on." I knew better. I glanced at Lorraine. She didn't know her husband as well as I knew my brother. I wondered what Francine had on Travis. It could be anything from women to . . . anything.

"It's a lot of money," Priscilla said baldly.

Lorraine turned toward her. "How much does she want?"

"She asked me for fifty thousand," Priscilla said.

Behind me, I heard a heavy sigh and then the tinkle of breaking china. I swung around. Amanda sagged against the wall. The coffee cup I had filled too full for Edmond lay in a shattered pile amidst a widening swirl of coffee on the parquet floor. Amanda held her hands tight against her chest.

I hurried to her, slipped an arm around her shoulders. "Mandy, what's wrong?"

"The cup." She tried to bend down to pick up the pieces.

My arm tightened and I held her. "Amanda, are you sick? What's wrong?"

"My heart," she whispered. "It . . . sometimes it does this. I have a pill. In the kitchen. It will be all right. But the cup . . . it is one of the Limoges. The pieces . . ."

Megan came up beside us. She said over her shoulder to the others, "Amanda is ill. K.C. and I will see to her." Then gently, "Amanda, don't worry about the cup. I'll get it. You go with K.C. and get your medicine."

Amanda and I moved slowly, together, toward the door. I wanted to kick and smash all the stupid priceless objects in the elegant room. They were killing Mandy. She was too old to have to work as hard as she had this evening, dinner for nine, then the clearing up, and still on duty bringing coffee and cookies to the library. Goddammit, how old did she have to get before Mother would let her rest? Or would she have a chance to grow old, to be the old, old lady I teased her about?

We had to stop three times before we reached the kitchen. I helped her to her old black rocker.

"The drawer. The little drawer."

I knew which one she meant. It was a tiny watchpocket slim drawer in an old chest that sat just inside the pantry. It was Amanda's chest. Her personal chest. That had been clear to us as children. We could open the huge cupboards, rearrange the seemingly endless rows of pots and pans, but the chest was Mandy's and we must be invited before we touched it. That very exclusivity made it the focal point of the kitchen, exciting our childish fantasies. What *did* the bottom drawer hold? Why was the second drawer so hard to pull out? The little drawer was the most magical drawer of all. It was there that she put special treats, candy shaped like coins and wrapped in gold foil, tootsie rolls, and ice mints, and, greatest of all, the pack of cards she used for telling our fortunes. Kenneth and Sheila and Priscilla and I would watch with huge eyes as her fingers, moving so swiftly, would slap the cards into rows and, softly and sibilantly, for Mandy had her own taste for the dramatic, she would tell our fortunes, grand and glorious fortunes of journeys over the seas and wondrous loves, of mysterious strangers and dark adventure.

I pulled the drawer out and it was empty except for a vial of pills and her wedding rings which she always took off before she cooked. I hadn't expected anything else, but it was like walking through a gate which had always opened into a lovely garden and finding only weeds and dust.

I opened the vial and gave Mandy one of the tiny nitroglycerine tablets. She put it under her tongue then rested her head back against the rocker.

She often sat in the rocker on somnolent summer afternoons. I could remember finding her there and the slow drowsy squeak of the rockers. Now she sat so still, looking so small and old, and the rocker never moved.

Tears began to trickle slowly down her cheeks.

I bent close to her. "Mandy, what is it? Do you hurt? Shall I call Rudolph?"

She shook her head.

I reached out and grabbed up her hands. "Mandy, I am going to call Rudolph. He will meet us at the hospital . . ."

"No. No."

I could barely hear her.

"No," she said wearily, so wearily. "I will go up to bed." Then she tried to struggle up out of the chair. "But the dishes . . . and the coffee. Your mother doesn't like for the coffee to get cold. I must . . ."

"Damn the coffee. And the dishes. I'll take care of it. You need to rest."

"It's all right now," she said. "It's better now. The pain is better."

The kitchen door opened behind us and Megan came through. "Amanda," she asked quietly, "how are you feeling?"

Amanda nodded heavily. "Better, Mrs. Carlisle. Much better."

"Oh, that's good," Megan said quickly. "I've talked to Jason. He called his wife and she is coming. They will take care of the dishes. You mustn't worry about anything. The important thing is for you to rest."

"I think we ought to take Amanda to the hospital."

Megan nodded. "If she feels that she should go, then by all means. Although if it is angina . . ." Megan reached out and patted Amanda's shoulder. "Is there still any pain? Any sensation of squeezing?"

I looked from one to the other, remembering now that Megan was a volunteer at the local hospital.

Amanda shook her head. "It's all right now. The tablet always makes it go away. I'm just tired. So tired."

Amanda was insistent that we not call Rudolph. I gave way finally and she and I went upstairs in the back elevator that had been installed when old K.C. III's gout kept him from climbing the stairs.

Amanda was quiet as I helped her undress and slip into a white cotton gown and climb up into her high old-fashioned bed. Her room was on the third floor and looked out over the back garden. It was a nice room with an attached bath and it sparkled with cleanliness. I looked at the walls, covered with pictures of Rudolph and his family and of the four of us, Kenneth and Priscilla and Sheila and me.

There weren't many pictures of Sheila, of course. But there was one that suddenly caught my eye. I had never seen it before. That was odd. Had Amanda had the picture and not hung it until years later when I no longer came to her room? Or had it hung there all these years and I had not seen it? Refused, perhaps, to see it. I felt cold and sick. I remembered so well when that picture was made. It was just a few days before Sheila died.

The picture showed Sheila sitting on the boat dock at the lakeside house. She was holding a crayon and pointing at the heavy white plaster cast on her leg. The leg that Kenneth and I had broken, in Grace's view. I don't know who took the picture. Whoever it was had stood too far away to get a crisp clear picture. It was fuzzy, a little out of focus, but you could see the squiggly markings on the cast. Everyone had signed it. Everyone but me. Sheila hadn't asked me.

It was frightful all these long years later to stand in Amanda's room and remember those two children, so twisted by hatred.

I had never admitted that before, but it was hatred that dominated our lives.

I wondered now, looking back at it, why this had been so.

Sheila hated me.

Why?

She was the golden child, the one my mother treasured. The rest of us paled in comparison. I never thought my brothers realized how little they and I actually mattered to Grace.

Sheila knew.

The picture was warped with age and it was black and white so it didn't show how Sheila's golden hair had glistened in the sunlight or the dark blue depths of her eyes—or the malice that peeked out of them at me.

The sudden touch of Amanda's hand on my arm made me jump.

"That picture," I pointed at it, "that picture, where did it come from?"

Amanda peered at it. "I'll take it down, Miss K.C., if it upsets you, but I thought it would be all right, after all these years. She was a sad child."

I looked at Amanda in surprise. Sheila a sad child? Surely Amanda didn't mean that. Or perhaps it was only the pity of age for youth that never bloomed.

"Where did the picture come from?" I asked stiffly.

Amanda looked away, wouldn't meet my eyes. "I found it," she said, her voice oddly defensive, "when . . . when I was going through some old boxes in the attic."

I started to ask what had prompted her to sort through the past but then I held back. She was old and her heart ached and perhaps it cheered her to remember days when she could work without stopping and the house buzzed with noise and activity, my brothers in and out, Sheila and I and, later, Kenneth and Priscilla, racing up and down the stairs—so long as Grace wasn't near.

"I believe I will go to bed now. Miss K.C.," Amanda said heavily, "it's time you went back downstairs."

"They won't miss me." I helped her up into the bed and leaned over to plump the pillows behind her head.

"Now, Miss K.C.," and her voice was sharp, "you go right back downstairs. They do need you. You can think better than any of them." She paused and sighed. "I knew your momma was upset but I didn't know . . . I had no idea what had happened. This Miss Boutelle, is she trying to hurt the family?"

I shrugged. "I don't know how much malice is involved. I'd say it's just the way she makes a better than average living. On the surface, she's an investigative reporter, but she's willing to sell back whatever really hot information she discovers. It's a nifty kind of blackmail."

"Blackmail . . ." Amanda moved restlessly and one hand plucked at the ribbon on her nightgown.

I realized suddenly and damn late that this wasn't the kind of thing I should be talking about. Here was Amanda, having an angina attack, and the best I could do was meander on about the Carlisles and their problems, most of which, to be brutally honest, they had created for themselves.

"Don't worry about it, Mandy," I said briskly. "It's not a life or death thing."

"Your momma, she's scared to death. Oh dear Lord. It's awful . . . so awful . . ."

"Hush now." I gently touched her lips. "You don't need to worry. We'll manage." I shrugged. "If she prints it, it won't be the end of the world."

"Miss K.C., Miss K.C.—" Amanda struggled to sit up. "I must tell you . . ." Then she sagged back against the pillows, a hand clutching at her chest, and gave a low moan.

I was scared. "Mandy, be quiet now, be quiet. You are making yourself sick again. Look, this is too much. I'm going to call Rudolph. He will come."

She lay back on her pillow, breathing hard. I called Rudolph and found him at home. When I told Mandy he was on his way, she nodded and rested with her eyes closed. I sat beside her bed, holding her hand, terrified that she was seriously ill, that she was going to die.

Megan knocked on the door, then came in and asked softly how Amanda felt. I told her I had called Rudolph and he was coming.

"That's good," Megan whispered. "K.C., they want you downstairs." She was frowning, her eyes troubled. "I don't understand what's happening. Kenneth didn't . . . tell me about this woman. He is refusing to have any contact with her and the rest of the family wants you to handle it."

Amanda opened her eyes. "You go on down, Miss K.C. I'll be fine."

I didn't want to leave her. She was all that remained of the best in my life. Dad was gone. I didn't want to leave her, looking so small and ill on the big bed. "I want to stay and hear what Rudolph says."

"I'll stay with her," Megan offered.

"You go down now." Amanda spoke so wearily, as if she were a long way away. It was a sound I had never heard in her voice before. Was she frightened? Did she think she was going to die? Amanda was brave. I knew that. She had lived bravely. She wouldn't despair at the end. I hesitated. Her dark eyes held mine for a long moment, then she nodded at me. I understood her unspoken command.

"I'll come back in a little while," I said.

I went downstairs because Amanda expected it of me.

They were going at it hot and heavy when I came in. Everyone, of course, had a different idea as to what should be done. I quelled them finally, but I didn't tell them what I really intended to do. I was going to handle Francine Boutelle, but I was going to do it my way—and not in a way I intended to publicize.

"Give me until Thursday morning," I insisted. "Put her off when she calls you, make some excuse, but don't set up any appointments until the end of the week."

If they had followed my advice, a great deal of trouble would have been avoided.

Edmond was skeptical from the start. "It will be ineffective to talk to that woman. The only solution is to buy the magazine."

I shrugged. "Start buying if you want to, Edmond, but keep your mouth shut about it. If Boutelle found out, she would just laugh and offer the article somewhere else."

Everyone agreed finally, at least on the surface, to let me handle Francine until Thursday. After that, it was anyone's game.

I had intended to settle it quickly but it was almost an hour before I could disengage and hurry back upstairs. Amanda's door was closed and Megan sat on a chair in the hall.

"How is she?"

"Sleeping. Rudolph came. He gave her a sleeping pill. He said she was doing all right and didn't need to go to the hospital but he's called a nurse to come for the night. I'm waiting for her."

"Does Rudolph think she is going to be okay?"

Megan nodded. "Don't worry, K.C. She just worked too hard tonight. And she seems upset about something but she didn't want to talk. Rudolph said she was very tired and needed to rest."

I nodded and thanked Megan and asked her to tell the night nurse I would talk to Amanda tomorrow. I left Megan at Mandy's door. I didn't go in to see her. I didn't want to disturb her. I thought, of course, that I would see her in the morning.

SEVEN

I woke John Solomon up on Tuesday morning. A nippy wind scudded paper cups and soiled newspapers down the alley. It was eight o'clock but the sun hung behind thin grey clouds. John's face sagged in folds like a dewlapped frog. He grimaced.

"The office opens at nine."

"So does mine. John, I need more help."

He gave an elephantine sigh. "The coffee's made. Come on in."

He shuffled ahead of me, pointing me vaguely toward his office while he disappeared down a short hall to the right. In a moment, he returned with a tray and two mugs with wreaths of steam curling over the coffee.

"Thanks, John."

He slumped into his chair, loaded his coffee with four packets of sugar and took a deep drink.

"K.C.," he observed mildly, "you are becoming a pain in the ass."

"I'll pay you enough that you can take your daughter to Lake Tahoe."

"I'd just lose money in the casino."

"How about Disneyland?"

"She's seventeen."

"Invite her boyfriend to go, too. They'll love you, Pops."

He managed a sour smile. "What do you need now?"

I told him.

He thought for a long time. "I don't want to lose my license," he said finally.

"John, that's not a problem. Just get me the equipment, that's all I ask."

"But the key?"

"It could be a key to anything."

"Breaking and entering."

"Breaking and entering what?" I replied quickly. "Don't ask me any questions. All you know is that you supplied me with some electronic gear—I could be planning on taping my niece's birthday."

"I didn't know you had a niece?"

"I don't."

"Hmm." He finished his coffee and tugged at the whitish stubble on his chin. "Hell, I haven't even shaved."

"That's all right. It's manly."

"Shut up." He took off his glasses, rubbed at his eyes then peered at me. "It will be expensive."

But he knew that didn't matter and, finally, he agreed.

"By noon," I stressed.

"All right, if I can manage it."

"You will."

The day, as usual, sped. Does any lawyer ever catch up? And, if I didn't bill some of my time pretty soon, my cash flow was going to be non-existent. There always seemed to be more important things to do than to bill.

I did try twice to call Amanda. Jason's wife, Ophelia, answered each time. "She's sleeping. Miss K.C.," and "I knocked, Miss K.C., but she tol' me to go on, she's restin'."

I decided that I would drop by the house in the afternoon. I needed to be sure that some additions were going to be made to the staff so that Amanda would have some permanent easing of her burden.

It was one-fifteen by the time I shook free from the office and went to John Solomon's. He had everything ready for me. It was expensive, but clever and worth every penny.

"It will fit a dozen places," John explained. "As for the other request you made, I can't provide anyone with means of opening locked doors. But, I suppose if someone happened to find a key on a floor somewhere and it just happened to be useful later . . ." He took a key off his desk, polished it quite carefully with his handkerchief and dropped it on the floor near my shoe. I bent down and picked it up and slipped it into the pocket of my blazer.

Once in my car, I took a small plastic recorder out of its soft bag and very carefully polished it, too. I had already put on a pair of leather gloves.

A block from Boutelle's apartment, I stopped at a drug store and used a phone in a back booth. Had she answered, I would have asked in a heavily accented voice if Quang Ngo lived there. It was one of the advantages of living in a community with a fair number of Vietnamese refugees.

There wasn't any answer.

I walked slowly back to the car, not eager now. It was easy to plan something like this, but the doing was another matter.

I parked around the corner from the apartment complex. I was wearing an all-weather coat, a dark brown scarf, sun glasses, and gloves.

I could be any woman between the ages of twenty and forty.

I walked briskly around the corner and into the first courtyard entrance. The apartments were built in a square with passageways at each corner leading into a central patio. Each apartment had its own interior entrance. I walked slowly on a flagstone path across the patio. It was chilly and dreary. Leaves fluttered into the empty swimming pool.

I saw no one.

I walked up to 14-D, took the key out of my pocket, opened the door and stepped inside. I closed the door behind me very, very gently and listened.

A clock ticked.

I stood in a tiny vinyl-floored foyer and looked up a narrow stairway. Then I looked to my left into the shadowy reaches of the living room.

It was dark and quiet, only the ticking of the clock breaking the silence.

I wanted frantically to hurry, to get my job done and get out, but I forced myself to wait and to listen.

The clock ticked.

Someone, of course, could be asleep in the upstairs bedroom but should anyone stir I should hear in time to get away.

Slowly, one step at a time, I moved into the living room. Then, with more confidence, I stepped into the kitchen. I unlocked the back door then hurried back to the living room. Now was the time to move quickly, to be done.

I looked quickly around the room and studied the possible hiding sites. Beneath the wide arm of a maple easy chair. In the corner behind the love seat. Behind the thick rough trunk of the rubber tree plant.

The rubber tree plant drew me. It was healthy, its wide curling fronds reminding me of the artificial greenery at a local cafeteria that ran to Polynesian decor.

I took the recorder out of my pocket, handling it gingerly. I really had no idea how it worked, but, according to John Solomon, it was set to start recording anything within a 10-foot radius at seven o'clock tomorrow evening. It would run for three hours.

It looked innocuous, a slender oblong box about the size of a typewriter ribbon spool box. The top was gridded. Tiny plastic buttons in an inset control panel regulated the recording. It was a marvelous product of miniaturization. You would think that a country that could produce such electronic marvels would be able to compete better in world markets. Then I saw the Sony label. Oh, well.

I tucked the recorder behind the rubber tree's trunk and used a swath of electrical tape to anchor it.

I was dropping the tape back into my purse when I sensed rather than heard movement behind me. I swung around, my heart thudding.

No one, nothing.

But I knew something had moved.

The clock ticked, outside the wind brushed a tree branch against a screen.

He jumped through the air to land on the couch. He stared at me with smoky blue eyes, his tail switching. Abruptly, he cried and the weird ah-yaah raised prickles on the back of my neck.

"Hello, fellow," I managed in a dry whisper.

The Siamese flicked back his ears and crouched.

I moved back a step. Where had he come from? From beneath a chair, from upstairs?

The front door hadn't opened. Had it? I craned my head but I couldn't see into the foyer. Then I heard the closet door in the foyer close.

I ran lightly, swiftly to the kitchen. As I pushed through the door, I heard her call, "Toby? Toby, where are you? Come here, kitty boy."

I didn't hesitate. I kept on going, slipping by the kitchen table, pulling open the back door. I slid outside and shut the door as quietly as I could.

Then I looked down. The damn cat was twining about my ankles.

Desperately, I grabbed him up, opened the door a fraction, shoved him inside, shut the door, then fled down the graveled walk.

I didn't relax until I was around the corner and hurrying to my car. My hands were damp on the steering wheel as I drove to Mother's. That had been too close. I hated to think how Francine Boutelle would have enjoyed catching me in her apartment.

But now I was in a position to turn the tables on her. If she didn't notice an intrusion in her house and make a search. If she didn't decide to water her rubber tree plant.

Would Francine notice that the back door wasn't locked?

No matter. I had done the best I could. Tomorrow night I would face her with what skill I could muster and hope for luck and arrogance. If I could get her talking, record blackmail in progress, well, then, Francine Boutelle might not be in the catbird seat.

I turned into Mother's drive. If it had seemed odd to be back last night, it seemed odder still to enter that familiar drive on a dreary October afternoon. Changes had been made. A freshly painted white fence marked the end of the parking area. Beyond it spread the rose garden. A pale pink marble nymph sat on a pedestal at the garden's center. When I was growing up, a metal stag forever reared on back legs there. I wondered when the nymph displaced him.

At the front door, I hesitated, rang the bell. Odd, too, to ring at a door where you once entered without thought.

No one came.

I waited several minutes, puzzled, rang again.

No one came.

Perhaps Jason's wife didn't hear well or was busy out in back, although garbage pails had long since been replaced by a trash compactor and the kitchen garden plowed under for grass.

I rang again, then, finally, turned the knob and entered.

The fountain splashed cheerfully in the tiled pool. The pale-rose Italian marble floor glistened with cleanliness.

"Mother?"

My voice echoed softly.

A door slammed at the back.

I began to walk down the broad hall with the Florentine paneling and the dark Spanish canvases hanging just above eye level. The swinging door from the kitchen burst open. Ophelia plunged toward me.

"Oh, Miss K.C." She looked relieved. "Is Amanda with you?"

"Amanda? No. I've come to see her. Isn't she in bed?"

Ophelia's face clouded. "Oh, Miss K.C., I don't know what to think. I took up a nice luncheon tray, with soup and an avocado and fresh tea, but she isn't there."

"Did you check the bathroom?" I asked, hurrying toward the stairs. "She may have fainted."

Ophelia trotted at my heels. "I looked in the bathroom, but she wasn't there. And she made the bed and her bathrobe and gown are in the closet."

I stopped and stared at Ophelia. "You mean she's dressed?"

"Yes. She's dressed and I can't find her anywhere."

Twenty minutes later I knew that Ophelia was right. The house was empty except for the two of us. Grace was at her Tuesday bridge luncheon and Jason was at his regular job at the La Luz Hotel.

"Perhaps she's gone into town, to Rudolph's office," I suggested though it seemed unlikely.

When I called, Rudolph was as puzzled as we. I called Rudolph's wife, Mary Kate. She was puzzled, then worried. "I talked to Mother this morning. She sounded tired and she promised to stay in bed all day. We were going to come and see her tonight. Where in the world could she have gone?"

I went back upstairs to Amanda's room. I stared at the high narrow bed, the coverlet drawn up over the pillows, tucked just so, as Amanda had always made any bed. I opened the closet. Her gown and robe hung on a hook to the right. Her clothes hung neatly from their hangers.

She had dressed, sometime before twelve-thirty, walked across the room and out the door to . . . Where could she have gone? And why? What could have called her out of the house? She was still weak, must still have been weak, from last night's attack.

Once again, I looked around the room. Such a simple shining room. A studio portrait of Rudolph, unnaturally solemn in his cap and gown, sat atop the narrow chest of drawers. The bulletin board, with its myriad pictures of all of us, hung next to the window. An old-fashioned footpress sewing machine sat next to a worn French Provincial desk that Grace gave Amanda the year the interior decorator redid the drawing room in Spanish baroque. Amanda was so proud of the lovely old piece. All she ever permitted on its top was her Bible.

Nothing lay atop the desk.

I walked slowly across the room. The desk top was bare.

Amanda had dressed and left, carrying her Bible with her.

I think I knew then.

I ran out of the house and pounded down the brick walk to the garage. The garage had been built for another era, the world of town cars and station wagons. I yanked up the first of the seven overhead doors and flicked on a panel of lights. All of the stalls were empty, including the last one where Amanda parked her Chevy.

She had driven away, carrying her Bible.

I ran to my car and drove, too fast, to the Paradise Valley Baptist Church and the cemetery that spread up the hill behind it. I knew where Amanda's husband was buried. I hurried up a twisting path to the plot bordered with a thin ridge of cement. A slender headstone carried the inscription, MORTON BRIDGEWATER, BELOVED HUSBAND OF AMANDA, B. 1905, D. 1945.

"Amanda?" As I called, fog began to swirl around the tree trunks, glisten against granite stones. "Amanda?"

A creaking wheel sounded behind me. I turned to see an elderly man pushing a wheelbarrow loaded with fresh dirt. I called out, "Have you seen a woman, an old woman, not very tall?"

How hard it is to describe someone you love.

He shook his head. "No ma'am. Nobody's come today. Nobody at all," and he looked at me curiously.

I walked slowly back to my car. The fog was thickening. As I drove out of the cemetery, I turned east on the narrow blacktop and I knew I was heading out of town, toward the lake.

It is a half-hour drive usually. Now, with the fog filling low ground like murky pools of silver, it took almost an hour. I turned in between the stone entrance pillars, my face grim, my hands sweaty on the wheel. I never came back without a feeling of depression and fear. I had rarely returned since that summer I was fourteen. The rest of the family continued to come but I went to camp and, later, to summer school. The fog helped. It danced and twirled ahead of me, making everything strange and different.

It could have been any country road, anywhere.

I didn't stop at the entrance to the wooden, two-story house, long since closed for the winter. I drove past, turned to the left and the road plunged down. The fog was so thick I switched on fog lights but I drove more from memory than sight. Then my heart gave a sickening lurch. Off to the right, shrouded in fog, sat Amanda's car.

EIGHT

"Amanda."

I shouted but the fog muffled my voice. The thin high sound fell away and there was only the slap of the waves pushing against the pilings of the pier and the uneasy rustle of the foggy woods.

"Amanda!"

No answer.

Hesitantly, I approached her car. The windows were rolled up. Of course, they were. Amanda wouldn't want the fog to drench the seat covers. She took good care of her car as she cared for everything around her. Tiny droplets of fog had condensed against the shiny brown paint. I peered inside. It was empty except for the old Bible on the front seat. The keys hung from the ignition.

"Oh, Amanda." I said it to myself, cried her name to myself. Filled with dread, I turned and began to walk toward the steps that led down to the pier. I was so afraid of what I would find—or not find.

Would the pier be empty? Was Amanda in that cold, cold water?

I knew the water was cold. And deep. It had taken the divers three days to find Sheila.

The fog pressed against me. I walked in a pulsing gray cocoon, able to see only a foot or two before me. I stepped out onto the pier and my shoes slapped hollowly. City shoes. Loud and out of place here.

As fogs often do, this one thinned for a moment and I could see, at the end of the pier, the rickety wooden bench with its tall slatted back. A small figure huddled there.

For an instant, hope surged. I began to run, calling out, "Amanda, Amanda."

The figure never moved. I stopped running, forced myself to walk. When I stood, looking down on her, I knew she would never move again, never smile at me with eyes full of love, never reach out work-worn hands to touch mine.

She wore her Sunday hat, a winter felt with a little wreath of blue velvet around the crown, and her best navy blue silk dress with a piping of white at the throat.

The silver of the shotgun, lying at her feet, shone with an obscene sparkle. The force of the explosion had blown it away from her hand. The front of her dress was torn and matted with blood.

I don't know how long I stood, staring down at the husk of the woman I had loved best.

Amanda, why?

I didn't cry. I felt too old and emptied to cry. I was facing something I could not understand, a horror that made no sense.

What could have driven Amanda to this bleak and lonely pier to end a good life, to end that life bloodily and brutally?

I stood there for a long time. It began to rain, a soft quiet rain. I couldn't bear to see the rain touch Amanda's face, splashing onto her dress to drain darkly down onto the wooden planking.

My scarf was sodden, my hair plastered against my head. I finally walked stiffly back to the house. The key was in the back door. Amanda, of course, had entered the house to get the shotgun from the gun rack in the study.

I called the sheriff's office from the phone in the kitchen. Then I called Rudolph. I told him as gently as I could but some news is not gentle, can not be gentled.

The afternoon seemed to stretch on forever; yet I could never later remember it clearly. The rise and fall of sirens. Cars, an ambulance. Men gathering at the pier, moving restlessly as flashbulbs exploded in the wet grey afternoon. Voices. Rudolph's face.

The sheriff turned to me at one point. "You found her, Miss Carlisle?"

"Yes."

"What made you think she might be here?"

I shook my head. "I don't know," I said dully. "I just came."

"She didn't say anything to you, the last time you saw her, that would help explain this?"

I remembered Amanda lying on her high bed, her face greyish with pain and fatigue, and her voice telling me sharply, "Now you go on downstairs, Miss K.C., they need you."

I had gone because she expected it of me. She took her responsibilities very seriously. I hadn't wanted to disappoint her.

Amanda's life had never been easy. She was widowed when just past thirty. Rudolph's sister, Essie, died of sickle cell anemia at fifteen. Amanda had no skills, no education, no opportunities, just determination and courage. She had made a good life for herself and her son.

What could have driven her to end that life?

Not ill health. Not Amanda. She knew illness. She would accept it as a burden but she would never give in.

What else was there in her life? She had devoted her life to her son and to the Carlisles.

"Miss Carlisle?"

The sheriffs voice brought me back.

"I'm sorry. Sheriff, I just don't know. She was sick but I can't believe . . ."

It did no good to say I did not believe. It had happened. Amanda had driven to a deserted lakeshore on a misty October morning and reached uncomfortably far to squeeze the trigger of a shotgun.

Time passed as it always does, no matter how joyful or dreadful the hours. It was all done, finally, and I was in my car driving back through the rain to La Luz.

It was dusk by the time I reached my apartment. When I unlocked the door, my shoe kicked an envelope that had been tucked under the door. When I picked it up and turned on the light, my hands began to tremble.

I recognized the handwriting. I had seen so many grocery lists in that firm looping script. Amanda wrote a fine hand for a girl who had had to quit school in the eighth grade and go to work to help her family.

I shut the door behind me and ripped open the envelope.

"Dear Miss K.C., I couldn't face the trouble I've made, but I want you to know I didn't mean to do it. That Miss Boutelle lied to me. She tricked me."

"Oh, Amanda," I said softly.

"I didn't know she was a bad woman," the letter continued. "She acted so nice and she told me your momma said I could talk to her. She said she was going to write a book about the Carlisle family and she was gathering material. I should have known it was funny she always came on Tuesdays when your momma was gone to bridge but I never thought. I talked to her five or six times and I told her everything but I didn't know she was going to turn and twist things to hurt you. She seemed to know a lot and I didn't pretend things were different than they were though I should have known your momma would never have told anybody about how Mr. Stephenson acted . . ."

Stephenson. I stared down at the letter. Stephenson? The name meant nothing to me. I didn't . . . Oh, Stephenson. Wasn't that the name of the interior decorator Mother had hired to re-do the city house five or six years ago? Larry Stephenson. It was while I was away at school. Amanda had mentioned him in a letter or two.

". . . but Miss Boutelle seemed to know all about him. Oh, Miss K.C., I told her so many things I shouldn't have, but the worst of all was about you and Sheila. I wasn't going to have it in a book that your momma thought it was your fault though you and I know she's always acted that way. But I knew better. I saw it happen that day. I never even told you that I knew because it hurt you so and you put it all away and never thought about it and I thought maybe that was the best. Sometimes, when things can't be changed and they are so awful, it's better not to think or talk about them. And now, that woman is going to put it all in a book and it won't sound right and it will bring it all back to you. I can't bear to be the one who hurt you, Miss K.C."

The writing was slipshod now, running off the ruled lines.

"Please, Miss K.C., forgive me. I didn't know what I was doing. I love you, Amanda."

Anger and grief swept me. I was going to destroy Francine Boutelle. One way or another. She was going to pay for what she had done. Oh Amanda, dammit, the Carlisles didn't matter that much. Not nearly that much. Who cared what Francine Boutelle wrote? It wasn't worth Amanda's little finger, much less her life.

I huddled in a chair in the living room, Amanda's letter clutched in my hands. Finally, tears came. I cried because I couldn't stop picturing Amanda's last morning. She was old and sick and upset, stricken by what she felt she had done to "her family." And she hadn't done anything wrong. She had been taken advantage of by a wily and experienced woman.

Amanda, why didn't you tell me? Why did you always try to protect me? Amanda, I could have told you it was all right.

All right? The old familiar feeling of fear swept me. I hadn't experienced the sweep of terror in many years. Amanda was right. I had buried that day when Sheila died so deeply in my mind that it was almost as if it had never happened—until this night of horror and grief. Now, once again, I was drowning, water slapping my face, water was in my eyes and nose and mouth, blinding and choking me as I struggled to swim on, to try and catch the little sailboat.

I could see Sheila's face.

Sheila was the prettiest sister. Everyone said that. She had hair the color of spun gold and eyes darkly blue as deep water.

Sheila's face wasn't beautiful then. It twisted with effort as she leaned far over the side of the little boat, holding the sail into the shifting wind, catching just enough power to stay out of my reach.

I tried to shout, to call her back, but I only made a strangled choking moan and I knew, at that moment, as I slipped again beneath the water, that my sister was going to drown me.

I had always been a little afraid of Sheila. Now, terror exploded in my mind, giving strength to failing arms. I flailed back to the surface, bobbing up on top of the cold deep water. Oh God, the boat was farther away. I couldn't swim to it. I couldn't reach it. Sheila, why are you trying to kill me?

The sail sagged into itself. The darting summer breeze had shifted enough that the sailboat hung in the water, not moving now. There it was. Dead in the water. Six feet away. Only six feet.

My legs were heavy, heavy, my lungs ached, water burned in my throat. My rubbery arms clawed at the water. I made a foot, another. My heart thudded and my eyes misted with effort. Water slapped up into my face and over my head and I began to sink. I gave a desperate frantic kick and slowly, more slowly than a heavy door closes, I rose through the water and broke the surface and gasped for air.

Sheila was struggling to swing the boom, trying to capture another puff of wind. She leaned awkwardly to the right, pinioned to the slick slanting deck by her right leg, encased in a heavy cast since her fall from the ballroom window.

I could barely see her, my eyes bleary with pain and fatigue. I wanted to cry out, "Sheila, I didn't make you fall. I would have fallen. You used the rope to go ahead of us. It wasn't there to hurt you. Sheila, why do you hate me so?"

I could only make a desperate sound deep in my throat. She heard it and turned to look over her shoulder and her blue eyes were as cold as alpine ice and as merciless.

I reached out, one weak stroke, another. Oh God, the boat was there, just ahead. If I could . . .

Sheila swung the boom in a quick vicious jerk. The wind caught it, the sail puffed like a cobra's hood, the boat lurched unevenly and Sheila began to topple over the edge. She grabbed at the boom but it was out of reach. She began to slide and then she was over the edge. She splashed heavily into the water, the cast pulling her down.

She sank like a stone.

The untended sail lost power and began to flap. The boat sat in the water. Slowly, heavily, one agonizing stroke after another, I struggled through the water until I could reach out and grab the boat.

I hung there until a boat came from shore. I hung there and stared at the water where Sheila went down.

I never told anyone what happened.

Was it because I didn't think anyone would believe me?

I don't think so.

It went deeper than that. I didn't want to admit that my sister had tried to kill me. I would wake in the night, screaming, but I never told anyone.

I never quite trusted anyone again.

Because I had never, until that moment, recognized Sheila's enmity. If my sister could will me to drown, what might the world do to me?

I never told anyone and I never quite trusted anyone.

It was an accident, everyone said, an unfortunate accident that claimed the life of the younger Carlisle daughter. Such a sad thing.

I huddled in the chair.

The doorbell rang.

I heard it but I didn't try to move. I shivered. The cold from the rain mingled in my mind with the cold darkness of the lake water.

The door opened. Greg called, "K.C., where are you? Your car's here. K.C. . . ." Then he stood over me.

"K.C., I'm sorry," he said gently. "I heard over the car radio, about your finding Amanda, and I came directly." He knelt beside me, put his arm around me. "Hey, you're wet and cold. You need a drink and a hot bath."

He drew the bath, laid out my gown and robe, brought me a scotch and soda.

I lay in the hot water and even managed to smile a little as I heard his muffled shout through the door, "Where the devil do you keep the coffee?" And, "Don't you ever stock your refrigerator?"

By the time I was dressed and warm and getting a little color back in my face, he had dinner ready, steaks and potatoes done in the microwave and a makeshift salad of cottage cheese and canned peaches.

"I can tell," he said severely, when I took my place, "that cooking is not one of your talents."

"I like to eat out," I said mildly.

"I don't," he replied immediately. "So that will be among the first changes."

I smiled at him, not ready to argue, and really appreciating his help this night. He had come and I had needed him.

After dinner, he insisted on putting the dishes in the dishwasher, settling me on the couch with an afghan and brandy.

Then he let me tell him.

For the first time in my life, I told the truth about Sheila.

"You poor little kid," he said gently.

I told him about Amanda and my voice shook with anger before I finished.

"God, that is rotten, K.C."

"Francine Boutelle is going to pay for Amanda."

Greg frowned. "What can you do?"

"I don't exactly know," I said evenly, "but somehow, someway, I am going to make Francine Boutelle just as miserable as I can."

"How?"

"For a starter, I'm going to fix it where she will never be able to sell a line to a reputable newspaper or magazine."

"The only way you can do that," he said slowly, "is to be willing to throw your family to the wolves."

"Damn the Carlisles," I said bitterly.

"Even if you do, I don't see how you can prove . . ."

"I can do it."

"This Boutelle woman will get very cagey if she gets any inkling what you're after."

"I'll talk to her as smooth as honey until I have it all down on tape, every damning word of it."

"Tape?" he asked sharply.

"That's right. Little Miss Francine doesn't know it but I've bugged her damn living room." I laughed. "She's in for a surprise, Greg. I've put the neatest little recorder you've ever seen right in the shadow of her rubber tree plant and tomorrow night at seven p.m. that little jewel is going to start running and I'm going to be there, leading clever Miss Boutelle into a trap she'll never get out of."

"Once you have the tape . . ."

"I won't be so charming," I said grimly. "The first thing I intend to do is send a copy of that tape to *Inside Out.* If that doesn't get her fired, I'll buy the damn magazine. I will also send that tape to every newspaper and magazine up and down the Coast. Francine Boutelle is going to rue the day she ever heard of the Carlisles."

It was quiet for a long moment. Greg was frowning.

"I'm sorry," I said finally, "if you don't find me too charming, Greg, but Amanda was old and helpless and . . . and nice . . . and that woman killed her."

He reached down, pulled me to my feet and wrapped his arms around me. "Hush now, K.C. It's all right. Don't get upset all over again."

I pulled free and walked to the mantel and reached out to grip it with taut hands. Greg didn't understand. Not really.

He came up beside me. "Look, K.C., you're too emotionally involved to handle this thing. Let me go and talk to this woman. Represent you. I'll scare the hell out of her and . . ."

I shook my head and answered quietly enough. "No, Greg. This is something I have to do. But I promise you, I can handle it. I will handle it."

NINE

Greg called early the next morning, still concerned about my appointment with Francine Boutelle. "It worries me. Obviously, she's a tough bitch and . . ."

"I can handle it. Remember, Greg, I'm a lawyer, too."

"Sure. But you aren't used to dealing with really sleazy people. It's like fighting a skunk, K.C., you can't come out smelling sweet."

It was nice, I suppose, that he wanted to protect me. I wasn't interested in protection.

"Don't worry, Greg. I can handle it," I repeated.

He sighed. "All right. If that's the way you feel. I'm going to a fundraiser but I'll try to get home early. Call me when you get home."

"Right."

I didn't spend the day stewing about it. I felt, in fact, cold and confident. La Boutelle didn't know what was in store for her. I felt even better after I talked to Pamela Reeves around five.

I didn't recognize Pamela at first when she walked into my office. Instead of her customary reddish brown hair, her head was topped by tight platinum curls. I looked at her speechlessly.

She grimaced. "You have a lot of control, K.C. John Solomon laughed like a hyena. My mother broke into tears. My little boy hid his face."

"Hmm. What . . . uh . . . prompted . . . ?"

"I have a precarious hold on my self-control. The smallest nudge may push me over the edge." She glared at me balefully. "It's all your fault."

"My fault?"

"Trying to get the goods on that damn Boutelle woman."

It turned out that Pamela had tracked down Francine's hairdresser. As any woman knows, the way to a hair stylist's heart is through her pocketbook. Pamela signed up for the A Number One First Class bleach job which took two hours. In two hours, it is possible to learn a great deal about a beautician's customers, their sexual preferences, social pretensions, and career aspirations.

"What did you find out?" I asked eagerly.

"Francine is madly in love."

"Who is he?"

"Clairabel was vague on that but he is, according to Francine, a really big deal. Handsome, exciting, a man on the move."

"Francine didn't mention his name to Clairabel?"

"No."

"He must be married."

"Why do you think so?" Pamela asked.

"It isn't natural for a woman to be so damn circumspect with her beauty-shop operator. You know how women talk. It's unconscious. George said this. George and I are going to the lake. George is so exciting."

Pamela shrugged. "If you make your living exploiting other people's private lives, you might be a little secretive about your own."

I was sure there was more to it than that. The identity of Francine's lover might be just what I needed.

"I don't care what you have to do to find out, but find out quickly. Put more operatives on it."

"K.C., your bill is already . . ."

"It doesn't matter."

When Pamela left, I considered calling Francine, putting off our meeting until later in the week. But I had the tape recorder in place, ready to roll at seven o'clock. It would be taking too big a risk to try and get it back, then plant it for another evening. After all, the important thing was to get our conversation down on tape, a clear-cut attempt at blackmail. That was the way to fry Francine's goose.

At seven p.m. I was sitting at my breakfast-room table, toying with a salad and watching the second hand sweeping around the kitchen clock. Had the tiny recorder hummed into action? Was it even now recording the slam of a door, the squeak of a chair?

My appointment with Francine was at eight. I left my apartment at twenty minutes before the hour. I wasn't able to park as close as I had Tuesday afternoon. The night was damp and raw. I pulled my all-weather coat closer, ducking my head into the whippy little wind. When I reached the courtyard, it was much warmer, the wind blocked by the building.

Light spilled cheerfully from Francine's front bay window. I pushed the doorbell.

No one came.

I jabbed the bell again, held it longer. Come on, Francine, I'm ready for you.

Maybe the bell was broken.

I knocked, hard. The door moved inward under the pressure of my knock. I gave the door a push, then jumped back, startled, as her cat flashed through the narrow opening and out into the night.

Why was the door ajar? What had frightened the cat?

I stepped into the foyer, still intent upon confronting Francine, trapping her. I looked into the living room where a lamp shone brightly.

"Francine . . ." My voice died in my throat.

The living room was a shambles, papers dumped out of the desk, books strewn on the floor. I looked past the disarray to a love-seat. A silly name for an odd-sized piece of furniture. Not comfortable for making love but called a love-seat. Meant for two people. Sitting upright. Francine was not sitting upright. She took up almost the whole seat, sprawled backward, her long sleek blond hair shining in the lamplight, her head tilted at an impossible angle, her arms flung backward, her legs spread gracelessly wide.

She was very, very dead.

My eyes jumped away from her face, mottled and bluish. Her tongue protruded dreadfully from her half-open mouth. Red and black bruises marked her throat.

Nausea swept me. I stood dumbly in the living room doorway, appalled and sickened.

How dreadful. How horrible.

I wanted to turn and run.

Instead, I stood rooted, unable to look away, the soft cerise of the expensive silk dress an awful contrast to her swollen and disfigured face.

I must call the police.

I moved, one leaden foot after another, toward the telephone which sat on the desk so terribly near that sprawled dead body.

It was going to be awkward for me to explain why I was here. What was I going to tell the police? Not, of course, that I had come, hoping to trap Francine Boutelle in the act of blackmailing me on a tape . . .

Oh my God. The tape recorder. I must get it. I couldn't tell the police about the tape recorder.

I swung around, hurried to the rubber tree plant. I was pulling the leaves apart, reaching for the recorder when the harsh command came.

"Turn around."

It startled me so much that I stumbled into the stand holding the plant and bruised a knee. Frantically, I whirled around, at the same time trying to back away.

My sense of fright lessened. He didn't look dangerous.

Frightfully sure of himself, perhaps. Accustomed to command. But not, surely, a murderer running rampant.

"Who the hell are you?" he demanded.

I took a deep breath, my heartbeat began to slow.

"I might ask the same of you," I replied.

He glared at me, his grey eyes icy beneath thick black brows. He was fortyish. A successful fortyish in a tan cashmere jacket, a yellow polo shirt, and dark brown slacks. His face could have been handsome except that he obviously didn't spend his spare time practicing ingratiating smiles before the mirror. He had a tanned lean face with a strong nose and black hair flecked with silver.

He wasn't looking at me now. He was looking at Francine. He didn't change expression. That made him all the more forbidding.

His eyes swung back to me, looked me up and down but without the subtle reflection of admiration I could usually expect from a man. He looked over my shoulder at the rubber tree plant. Without a word, he strode across the room, moved past me and pulled down a thick green front. He studied for a long moment the shiny black plastic recorder taped to the rubber tree trunk.

"How did you know it was there?" he demanded.

So he went right to the point.

I lifted my chin. "I heard a humming noise. I wanted to see what was causing it."

He bent his head a little, listened.

There was no humming noise.

Those icy grey eyes looked at me again.

"Carlisle," he said abruptly. "K.C. Carlisle."

It was my turn to look sharply at him.

I didn't know him. I was sure of it. He was not a forgettable man. I was quite sure I had never met him.

"What are *you* doing here?" he asked.

I hesitated, then answered. "I had an appointment with Miss Boutelle. I came. The door was open. I found her."

"You walked right in?"

"I knocked. The door came open. I expected her to be here so I stepped inside—and this is what I found."

We both looked again at the couch.

"Have you called the police?"

"No. I was going to . . . and I heard that humming noise."

I certainly hoped John Solomon and I had polished that recorder well enough because now I had a story and I was stuck with it. It could have been true.

"Who are you?" I asked abruptly. I would prefer that this obviously intelligent man not think too long about that recorder.

"Harry Nichols. I own *The Beacon.*"

That laid it on the table all right.

So this was Harry Nichols, who didn't like the Carlisles. Of course, it was his father who had begun the vendetta. But he had continued it, witness the attacks on Kenneth during the campaign.

We looked at each other warily.

"How did you know me?" I asked.

"You were elected president of the Young Lawyers last month. I remember your photograph."

"It's nice to be memorable," I said pleasantly.

He didn't smile. "I was thinking about the Carlisles as I drove over here tonight."

"Really?"

He reached into his coat pocket and pulled out a letter. "This came in the mail this morning." He tossed it to me.

I held it. "Do you want me to read it?"

He nodded.

It was concise, pointed, and, for Kenneth, unfortunate as hell.

Dear Mr. Nichols,

If *The Beacon* wants the real low-down on what kind of person Kenneth Carlisle is, so the voters can be protected, come to my apartment tonight at eight-fifteen.

It was signed by Francine Boutelle in a flashily flowing script.

I folded the letter, slipped it back into the envelope.

"And, of course, with the *Beacon's* known fondness for the Carlisles, you came hotfoot."

He didn't rise to it. "I came. I didn't know what to expect." He looked again at Francine. "I didn't expect this."

"Neither did I," I said wearily.

He called the police, carefully using a handkerchief to hold the receiver and a pen to move the dial. We waited five minutes for a patrol car and twenty minutes for the detectives.

Arrivals and departures continued over the next hour, the medical examiner, several squad cars, the photographic unit, more detectives, and finally, an ambulance. I didn't watch as the expressionless young men swiftly rolled Francine onto the cart, slipped over a canvas cover, and wheeled her out into the night.

Harry Nichols and I waited in the foyer, in the way, but not, of course, free to go.

"Did you know her well?" he asked me.

I shook my head. "Not at all. I had met her once."

"Had you ever met her?" I asked a little later.

"No."

"So you came because of the letter, hoping to scare up some scandal against Kenneth."

He wasn't defensive. "Not precisely, Miss Carlisle." He looked at me dispassionately. "I wouldn't have minded learning something embarrassing to Carlisle." For a moment, Nichols looked exasperated. "Going after your cousin isn't especially easy, Miss Carlisle. He is too rich and successful to be involved in anything disreputable. The most you can say about Kenneth Carlisle is that he will bore you to death."

That stung me to a reply. "Then why do you attack him, day after day, Mr. Nichols?"

"He is Robert Carlisle's son. As far as I'm concerned, that will always be reason enough."

"Not a particularly defensible position, I would think."

"I don't ever find it necessary, Miss Carlisle, to defend my positions."

He was so sure of himself. Answerable to no one. A bad enemy.

Another siren cut through the night to die in the street outside. Through the propped-open door, I saw a man get out of the back of yet another police car and start up the walk.

It was clear, the way other police scurried around him, that this man was in charge.

"Who's that?" I asked Harry Nichols.

He looked past me and his eyes flickered with interest.

"That's Nelson Farris. Chief of detectives."

Farris was tall and bulkily built. He wore dark slacks and a navy pullover sweater. As he came nearer, I saw that his face was blunt and hard. He wore his hair in a fairly long crew cut. He looked tough and competent.

Farris moved past us into the living room. The men there reported to him. Then a chubby-faced patrolman turned and pointed toward us.

Farris' dark, heavy-lidded eyes studied us for a moment. He began to walk toward us.

I felt a rush of fear.

TEN

"I want to talk to you." Farris's voice was hoarse and tired. Too many cigarettes and too much whisky for a lot of years. "Let's go into the kitchen where it's a little quieter."

We followed him, stepping carefully around the paraphernalia of the cameramen and fingerprint experts. One man, on his hands and knees, was slowly scooting a small vacuum cleaner around the base of the love seat.

My mind was a frantic whirl of indecision. I could not, of course, lie to the police. But, on the other hand, I was under no compulsion to tell everything I knew. How to balance the fine line between deception and minimal cooperation was going to take a lot of judgment.

Farris motioned us to sit in the booth opposite the kitchen range. Harry Nichols politely waited for me to slide in first, then he sat beside me. Farris took his place across from us. He pulled out a small notebook and a pen from his briefcase.

For a long moment, it was absolutely quiet in the kitchen as Farris looked at us.

"Anything you say may be used in evidence against you," he said abruptly. His raspy voice reminded me of a cat clawing a screen. "You have the right to have a lawyer present."

The Miranda warning. I recognized it for what it was, a necessary protection to the investigation, a formality to keep evidence untainted. Still, it was a shock to hear it.

Nichols was shaking his head impatiently.

Farris looked at me. "Miss Carlisle?"

"No." My throat felt dry and parched. "No, I don't need a lawyer."

"All right then. I understand, from Patrolman Fisher, that you found the body. How did it happen?"

I knew that he assumed we had come together. I wanted to get my piece out first, before Nichols spoke.

"I had an appointment with Miss Boutelle at eight o'clock. I rang the doorbell. She didn't come so I knocked. That pushed the door open and her cat came running out. I thought that was odd. I called out and then I stepped into the foyer. I saw the mess in the living room so I walked in there—and found her."

Farris looked from me to Nichols and back again. "You weren't together?"

"No," I said quickly, "but Mr. Nichols must have been right behind me."

Farris turned to Nichols. "Did you see Miss Carlisle enter the apartment?"

"No."

"So she could have been inside for some time before you came?"

"No," I interrupted sharply. "I had just arrived. I only had time to find her and then I thought I heard a humming noise . . ."

"Humming noise?" Farris asked.

Nichols and I both told him and Farris was on his feet and out of the kitchen before we finished.

We heard him explode. "How the hell could you miss it?" he demanded. "What the hell else have you missed? Fritz, get over here. Get some pictures, fingerprint it, then bring it to me.

When he returned to the kitchen, he looked at me dourly. "You heard a humming sound?"

"I thought I did," I said doubtfully.

"Funny. It was still running—and I couldn't hear a thing."

I didn't say anything.

"Did you touch it?" he asked.

"No." Sweat beaded my mouth. Had I polished it well enough the afternoon that I brought it here? "You can ask Mr. Nichols. He came in just as I found it."

Nichols nodded agreement.

Farris looked at both of us with impartial dislike. "Machines don't hum for a while then stop humming. If you heard it humming, it should still be humming."

"Maybe I was mistaken."

"But you found it?"

I nodded warily.

His dark eyes stared hard at me. "What is it, Miss Carlisle?"

I hesitated, but the answer seemed obvious. "I would guess that it is some kind of tape recorder."

"You would guess that?"

"Yes."

"Miss Carlisle," he rasped, "let me give you a little advice."

I ventured a small stiff smile. "Of course."

"Why don't you tell me what you were really doing here?"

I simulated surprise. "Captain, I've told your men the truth and I'm sure it can be verified at Miss Boutelle's office. She was working on an article about the Carlisle family and I had an appointment to discuss it with her."

"A friendly meeting?" he asked silkily.

I knew then that despite his craggy face and tough demeanor, he had a feline streak—and that would make him doubly dangerous.

"I never assume an interview will be either friendly or unfriendly until it occurs, Captain."

His mouth twisted in disgust. "They must teach it in law school."

"Pardon me."

"This either-or crap." Brusquely, he began to bounce questions at me.

"What time did you leave your apartment tonight?"

"Around twenty to eight."

"What time did you get here?"

"A few minutes before eight."

"Tell me exactly what you did, from the time you left your car."

A stolid-faced young man with a stenographer's notebook sat on a straight chair a few feet away. He was taking down everything that was said.

I'd better, from now on, remember what I said here.

I told it just the way I had to the patrolmen who arrived first.

"What did you touch?" Farris asked.

New ground here. Be careful, K.C.

"The front door," I said slowly. "The lower leaf of the rubber tree plant."

"Nothing else?"

I felt a touch of panic. Had I touched anything else that afternoon that I left the recorder? Oh God, the back door. There was no way I could explain prints on the back door! Then, sweet relief that left me limp, yet trying hard not to reveal any of the emotions that had swept me. I didn't need to worry. I had worn gloves on Tuesday.

Had that instant of panic shown on my face?

Farris was waiting for my answer.

"I don't believe," I said slowly, cautiously, "that I touched anything else."

"You don't believe so?" he mimicked.

"No."

He asked abruptly. "Do you know of any reason why anyone would kill Miss Boutelle?"

Reason? I knew several, but I looked at him blankly. "I'm sorry, Captain. I know nothing of Miss Boutelle's private life."

It was an oblique answer but he didn't notice.

"Did you kill her?"

"No."

He turned to Harry Nichols. I didn't listen too closely. I knew what Nichols was going to say. I reviewed in my mind the answers I had made. I had better remember them, repeat them the next time the questions were asked.

Then Farris turned on me again, his tone sharp. He held out the letter Nichols had received. "What do you know about this?"

"Nothing."

"What do you mean, nothing?"

"Exactly that."

His face hardened. "You expect me to believe it's some kind of coincidence that you find the body of a woman who has just written a threatening letter about your cousin?"

"My visit here had nothing to do with that letter."

Farris glared at me, but I've been around too long to be quailed by a glance. He gave it up, finally, and turned back to Nichols.

"Is this letter the only contact you've had with Miss Boutelle?"

As Harry Nichols nodded, a plainclothesman brought the recorder in and handed it to Farris. "It was running. We stopped it."

Farris took it. He looked at me for a long moment with dark suspicious eyes. "Shall we play it back, Miss Carlisle?"

"That's fine with me."

His index finger flicked the tiny button and we all could hear the tape whirring. It ran and ran and a tiny flag of excitement waved in my mind. By God, the tape had worked or there wouldn't have been any tape to reverse. But I wasn't supposed to know anything about this recorder or when it had begun to record so I tried to look merely interested.

Finally, the whir stopped. Farris pushed the play button.

Listening to the tape was an eerie experience. It opened with a bell clock chiming seven o'clock. Behind the soft bell tones, there was a ragged whistling noise that none of us identified for a long moment. Then, sickeningly, I realized we were hearing the gasping breaths of someone under great emotional stress. There was a sound of movement, impossible to define, hurried footsteps, the slam of a door.

The tape whirred on and on with no sound, only the faint hiss of its own movement.

Farris speeded it up, dropped it to normal when the doorbell rang. A door opened, then there was a long silence. A dull sound of movement, then, finally, a door slammed.

Again there was silence. Minute after minute of silence.

No voices. Nothing. I pictured Francine on the love seat, eyes bulging, tongue protruding.

The front door bell rang on the tape. It rang again, longer. Then a knock.

"Francine . . ." It was my voice, dying in shock.

Farris glanced at me.

My footsteps, hesitant, reluctant, faintly sounded.

"Turn around." No mistaking that voice, that tone of command.

Farris let the tape run on until it picked up the sounds of the arriving police. When he turned it off, I attacked.

"I have told you the truth. The tape proves it."

"You could have left and come back," he replied.

He dismissed us then.

On the way out, I tried to see if there was anything lying about that looked like a manuscript.

Farris was coming along behind me. "Looking for something, Miss Carlisle?"

"No," I said coolly, "I'm merely curious, Captain. I've never been this close to the scene of a crime before."

I'm sure my answer confirmed Harry Nichols's opinion of the Carlisles in general and me in particular, but Farris undoubtedly brought out the worst in me.

But Nichols was more interested in what he had managed to discover as we walked through the living room. On the steps outside, he asked, "Did you see the cassettes stacked in the bookcase behind her desk?"

In the milling confusion, I had missed that.

"They were labeled," Nichols continued. "I would guess she worked on tape."

That hadn't occurred to me, though I suppose it should have from her actions at my office. Her search for a hidden tape recorder would indicate someone accustomed to using tapes. So the absence of a manuscript didn't mean a thing. Francine may have taped for posterity all the dirt she had on the Carlisles and a police technician might soon be hearing all about us.

"That worries you?"

I would have denied it but he was too perceptive by far.

"I would be interested to know what's on them," I responded.

We were at the sidewalk now. We stopped, looked at each other and Nichols said abruptly, "I've got to get to a phone to call our police reporter." He paused, then said slowly, "I'll ask him to see what he can find out about the cassettes."

Was he actually offering to help me? "I would appreciate that."

Nichols frowned, his dark brows drawn tightly together. "There's a bar a couple of blocks from here. We could get a drink and I'll call him."

A Carlisle having a drink with a Nichols. It had an unholy aura

I couldn't resist. I could find out more about the murder through Nichols and *The Beacon*. Of course, I'd better not forget who he was. He obviously guessed there was more to my appointment with Boutelle than I had revealed.

"I'd like a drink," I said finally.

We took my car. Louie's was a quiet neighborhood bar with Streisand and Simon and Garfunkel and Joan Baez on the juke box, a pocket out of yesterday. We were Harry and K.C. by the time we slipped into a back booth.

After we ordered, Harry went to the pay phone back in a dingy hall between the restrooms. I slowly sipped a margarita and debated trying to call Kenneth. But I needed to be careful. It might endanger Kenneth more if he knew about Francine's murder when Farris came to see him.

I wished I had a legal pad with me. There is something so clarifying about laying out a problem on the familiar yellow sheets. And it would build a wall of words against the picture of Francine that hung in my mind.

I took a deep, deep drink.

When Harry slid back into the booth, he drank down half his drink before he said a word. "I got Paul Lowery. He's our police reporter. He gets along with Farris. If anybody can find out what's on those cassettes, it's Paul."

Then he stared at me, his face somber.

So he was going to help me.

I knew it would be better to leave it alone, but I had to know.

"Why are you helping me?"

For a long moment, I thought he wouldn't answer. Then, finally, he said wearily, "Life is damned odd. I would have sworn I would never do anything for a Carlisle. And yet . . ."

I waited.

He reached across the table suddenly, gently cupped my chin in his hand. "Goddamnit, you look so much like her."

His hand dropped away. I was suddenly aware that I liked his touch and, at the same time, I was oddly offended. I was K.C. Carlisle and I looked like myself.

"Like who?" I asked distantly.

He didn't notice my tone. He was staring down at the table, seeing things I could not.

When he talked, it was almost to himself. "She was a blonde, too. Tall and leggy. She was . . . she was beautiful and her eyes were dark like yours." He looked up at me. "But different. She had trusting eyes." His mouth twisted a little. "You don't trust anyone, do you?"

It was closer to the mark than I would admit.

"I know that I . . . idealized her." It was hard for him to say. I could hear the pain in his voice. "She was older than I, enough older that when mother died it was really Susie who raised me."

He saw the total bewilderment in my eyes.

"My sister," he said quietly. "My sister, Susie." He cocked his head, studied me. "The resemblance is in the way you hold your head, the way you move. I don't think you are much like her in personality. Susie was very outgoing and happy and . . . trusting."

My margarita tasted even more sour than usual.

He picked up on it immediately. "But you aren't that kind of person, are you?"

"No," I agreed, "I don't suppose I am an especially trusting person."

"Susie was trusting. And it killed her." He glared at me angrily and finished off his drink. "So what the hell am I doing here with you?"

"I don't know, I'm sure."

"I'll tell you about Susie."

I could have said I wasn't interested. But I was.

"How old are you?"

"Twenty-eight."

"You've slept around some."

It could have been offensive. Oddly, it wasn't. He didn't wait for me to answer. He answered it himself.

"Sure you have. You're a beautiful girl. A normal girl. Times are different now. When Susie was growing up, in the late fifties, no one was open about sex."

As he told it, it was a familiar enough story. A girl met an attractive older man. She fell in love with him. He was married. When she told him she was pregnant, he left town. Took his wife and went on a trip around the world.

"I understand he had a fine trip," Harry said huskily. "Played polo in England. Even bought some new horses for his string."

I knew then. I had heard a lot, growing up, about how well Uncle Bobby played polo.

"I didn't know," I said quietly. "I didn't know."

"She died the week before her twenty-third birthday," Harry said brutally, "in a goddam cheap sleazy boarding-house on Sausalito Street where she had gone for an abortion."

Now I knew why the Nichols hated the Carlisles.

I reached out, touched his hand tentatively. "I'm sorry, Harry. God, I'm sorry."

"You didn't know?"

I shook my head. If others in the family had known, no one had ever told me. And somehow I doubted that Kenneth knew this about his father.

"Uncle Bobby was..." I shrugged. "I guess the Victorians saw life pretty clearly. They had the best word for men like Uncle Bobby. He was a rotter." I hesitated, said gently, "Harry, he's dead. He's been dead for years."

Harry stared at me, his grey eyes dark with anger. "I was thirteen when Susie died. I swore that someday, when I was grown, I would kill him. But the mountains killed him first."

"Can't you let it go?" I asked. "Let it all go?"

"It isn't that easy," he said slowly. "I don't think the past is ever over. Ever."

I understood that. I, of all people, understood that. "You don't have to help me," I said abruptly and I started to slide out of the booth.

"No, K.C. Wait."

I looked at him inquiringly. "Don't leave."

"Don't leave."

"Are you sure?"

"Yes."

We ordered a second round and were awkwardly silent for a moment, then he asked me about college and law school and, gradually, we began to talk, as if we weren't a Carlisle or a Nichols, two people finding out about each other.

"Have you always worked for *The Beacon,*"

His life hadn't followed neat patterns, either. He spent a tour in Vietnam, was one of the early "advisers." When he was discharged, he spent a few years drifting from one big city newspaper to another. He didn't want to come back to La Luz and be the boss's son. Then his father died of a heart attack and he came home to *The Beacon.*

"Are you glad you came back?"

He nodded. " Mostly." He looked at me directly. "I got married then, too."

I waited.

"Two kids, Harry Jr. is a freshman at Dartmouth. Susie lives with me. She's fourteen."

"And your wife?"

"Ex-wife. She's married to . . . a former friend of mine."

So what do you say? 'I'm sorry.' 'I'm glad.' I didn't say anything.

"I'm back where I started. A bachelor. I intend to stay that way."

He said it angrily, bitterly. This was one divorce I wouldn't ask about.

"Going it alone is better," I said quickly. Maybe I almost believed it. It was the way I had lived for a long time.

Harry's face smoothed out. "That's enough about me. Tell me, K.C., why did you go to law school?"

I never had a chance to answer.

"Hey, Harry." The bartender was yanking a thumb over his shoulder. "Phone."

Harry went to answer. I finished my second margarita and decided that was enough. When Harry came back, I would thank him and offer him a ride back to his car. I needed to go home and do some thinking.

But when Harry came back, I knew from his face that something big had happened.

"I'm sorry, K.C. Sorry for you. Farris has arrested your cousin Kenneth."

ELEVEN

It fell into place for Farris, I later learned, as neatly as a cell door clanging shut. Maybe there is an instinct to the hunt, a subconscious nerve-twang, that prompts a detective to make a try, and, when it succeeds, he is acclaimed for his cleverness and it reconfirms his own confidence and sets in concrete his original perspective. Farris had the letter, of course, that damning letter that pointed to Kenneth. When one of his men returned to the apartment with the news that a neighbor had seen a man leaving Francine's apartment hurriedly just after seven, Farris went immediately to talk to her. The final piece of good luck and, from Farris' viewpoint, proper response to his seeking out, was the neighbor's description of the man, "Well, it looked like the young man who is running for the House. I've seen his ads on the TV. Carlisle, that's his name."

Farris was primed for bear and he wasn't new at the game so he took the time to roust out a judge and get a search warrant. He drove to Kenneth and Megan's house. It was dark, a night light burning in the bay window. Farris wasn't in any hurry. He settled back in his unmarked car and smoked and waited.

The Mercedes glided up the wide circular drive just before eleven. The garage door swung up automatically, the car pulled in and the door came down.

Farris and his assistant got out and walked up to the front door and rang the bell. Kenneth answered the door, still in the tuxedo he had worn to the symphony. Megan was just starting upstairs, her long dress a shimmer of silver in the light of the entry way chandelier.

It was about an hour after this that I drove up the steep street and turned into the drive. A police cruiser blocked the way. A policeman shone a light in my face. "This drive's closed."

"I'm going through. This is my cousin's house. I intend to talk to his wife."

He turned without answering and walked back to his cruiser and leaned inside to talk on the radio. I couldn't hear the exchange, but he returned in a moment to ask, "Are you K.C. Carlisle?"

"Yes."

"You can go through."

He backed his car out of the way and I edged by in the Porsche.

The house blazed with lights. Two more squad cars were parked by the front steps. The front door was open. I stepped into the entryway of pale green Italian marble. I could see my reflection in the gilt-framed mirror that hung above a Chippendale side table. My face glimmered at me, pale and strained.

A uniformed policeman sat uncomfortably on a spindle-legged chair. "Are you Miss Carlisle?"

I nodded.

"Mrs. Carlisle is in there," and he nodded towards the drawing room.

Megan waited for me just inside the double doors. She reached out to draw me through. "K.C., thank God you've come." She shut the doors. "They've arrested Kenneth. K.C., they've arrested him for murder."

Her eyes burned in a face paled by shock. The diamond necklace at her throat glittered in the light of the wall sconces. Megan clutched at her throat, oblivious to the necklace, frantic with worry.

"I know, Megan. That's why I've come. Tell me everything that's happened."

Footsteps sounded above us. Megan looked up at the ceiling. "They're still here. They are pawing through our things, looking everywhere."

"Do they have a search warrant?"

"Yes. They showed it when they first came. They found something in the trunk of Kenneth's car. I don't know what it was but they were all excited." She paused and looked at me with haunted eyes. "And Kenneth . . ." She said it slowly, it was hard to say, "Kenneth looked awful when they asked him for the keys. It was when they came back in from the garage that they arrested him."

I suddenly felt very tired. I knew what they were hunting for, of course. Any of the materials that were missing from Francine's desk. And, more than that, they were looking for whatever had been used to strangle her. It was Harry who had told me he was sure something had been used, a rope or a tie of some kind.

"Megan, where was Kenneth tonight, between six and seven?"

"Between six and seven?" she asked faintly.

I nodded.

"He called," she said dully, "about six and said he would be a little late getting home. He needed to finish a contract." She hid her face in her hands for a long moment. Her voice was muffled. "Oh, K.C., I called the office about six-thirty. I wanted him to stop on the way home and buy some Chablis . . ."

There wasn't any answer. "What time did he get home?"

Her hands dropped away from her face. I didn't look at her. It was too painful.

"About seven-thirty." Her hands knotted in fists. She continued reluctantly, "He was upset. I knew that. I always know when he is upset, when something is wrong. He said he had a bad headache, but he insisted we go on to the symphony." She looked at me forlornly. "K.C., what happened?"

"Have you told this to the police?"

She shook her head.

"Keep your mouth shut. If they want to talk to you, refuse to say anything unless I am present."

"All right, K.C."

I hesitated, but I had to ask it. "Megan, do you have any idea what Francine had on Kenneth?"

"No. But something has been wrong for weeks. Kenneth hasn't been himself. At night, we would be home, just the two of us, and I would look up and he would be looking at me . . . so strangely. When I would ask, he always said nothing was wrong. But K.C., I knew that wasn't true."

Yes, something was very wrong. Kenneth hadn't engineered the dissolution of the Cochran-Carlisle trust for nothing.

"Has it just been the past few weeks?"

Her mouth tightened. "Yes. I know what everyone will say. They will say he was having an affair and this woman found out and wanted money to keep it secret and he killed her because of me . . . or the campaign." She swallowed jerkily. "It isn't true. I tell you it isn't true."

The wife was always the last to know, wasn't that the folk wisdom?

I wouldn't know. I had never been married, never had a husband to lose. But I wondered if in this instance folk wisdom failed? Wouldn't you know, wouldn't you know instinctively if the man you loved had turned to another? Perhaps you could be fooled if he had always been untrue, but I felt sure that couldn't have been the case with Kenneth.

Kenneth loved Megan.

That was a constant, a basic, a given.

Wouldn't Megan have known?

She reached out, gripped my arm. "I tell you it can't be true, K.C. We . . . Kenneth and I . . . I tell you, it can't be true."

"All right, Megan," I said soothingly, "relax. Don't get upset." Wasn't that a laugh. Don't be upset, dear, just because they've arrested your husband for murder. "Let's sit down, Megan, think it out, pool what we know. It's the only way we can help Kenneth."

If Kenneth could be helped. I didn't say it, but I thought it. I asked what I had to know, "Megan, what did Kenneth say when they arrested him?"

We sat on the long couch beneath a vivid Van Gogh. I remembered when Kenneth and Megan bought the painting at an auction at Sotheby's. They had been so proud of it, in a well-bred way. Now the driven, tortured strokes in the painting seemed to echo the pain in her face.

"He just looked stricken. He turned to me and he tried to smile. It was . . . dreadful. He said, 'Megan, no matter what they say, I didn't do it.' Then that man, the police captain said it was time to go down to the station, they had a lot to talk about. Kenneth didn't even look at him. He just ignored him and stared at me and said, 'Megan, please, I love you,' and then he turned and walked out with all those men around him."

Kenneth was always such a perfect product of his background and breeding. For him to have spoken publicly, before the police, of love showed just how great the strain upon him.

I could imagine the words, almost see Kenneth's face. Of all who knew him, perhaps I alone knew how much he loved Megan. I didn't think, no matter what happened, that he would lie to Megan.

For the first time since Harry told me Kenneth had been arrested, I began to think in terms of Kenneth's innocence, not his possible guilt.

There could be an innocent explanation for all that had happened. If Kenneth had been at Francine's apartment, it didn't necessarily mean he was her murderer. I had been there and I hadn't murdered her.

I couldn't help Kenneth unless I knew more than I did now.

"Megan, tell me exactly when you realized Kenneth was disturbed about something."

She frowned. "It was almost exactly a month ago. He was late coming home from the office and he isn't often late. We were supposed to go to the charity auction at Ruisdael's that night. Kenneth had forgotten and that was so unlike him. We went and he didn't make an offer on anything. I made a bid finally on a weekend at La Jolla and Kenneth hardly had a word to say about it on the way home. Nothing was right after that evening. Kenneth would try hard to be happy, like we've always been, but then his face would look worried, distant. I didn't ask him. I thought surely he would tell me soon. But he didn't. Then I worried that it was another woman. It is so common, you know. So many people we know . . . but K.C., I can't believe it, I don't believe it. It wasn't that he didn't come home at night or didn't," she paused painfully, "make love to me. It wasn't that at all. He seemed, really, to love me more, to be more intense. It was more as though he had a dreadful fear." She pushed up from the couch and walked to the mantel to stare into the empty grate. "Then I was afraid, so afraid, that there was something terribly wrong physically. That he had cancer and he didn't want to tell me." She turned to look at me, her narrow chin high, "But Kenneth isn't a coward. Oh K.C., I haven't known what to think."

"I don't know what it could be, either," I said slowly.

"There is something," she said, her voice weary. "I've known it ever since the night at your mother's. I asked him on the way home if Francine Boutelle had asked him for money. He looked straight ahead and kept on driving and then he said he didn't want to talk about it, that I wasn't to worry. I knew then that he didn't want to tell me. I guess I was hurt. I didn't mention it again. I started talking about the campaign, about how well the contributions were coming in . . . He reached out and took my hand and held it so hard. I wanted to cry. But I didn't."

The Megans of this world don't often cry. They don't often ask for help, either.

"K.C., please, tell me, whatever it is, if you know. I can't help Kenneth if I don't know what he's fighting."

"I would tell you if I knew, Megan. All I can say for sure is that Francine Boutelle was a blackmailer. She tried to blackmail me and Priscilla. I'm certain of that. I think she had also threatened Grace and Travis and Edmond."

"The whole family?" Megan exclaimed.

For the first time in hours, I smiled. "The whole damn marvelous family."

"Not just Kenneth," Megan said eagerly.

"No. Not just Kenneth."

"So Kenneth isn't the only one with a motive, is he?" Megan demanded.

I hadn't thought of it like that. I looked at Megan with a new respect. Obviously, she didn't care what it took to clear Kenneth, including jettisoning someone else in the family.

"No," I agreed, "Kenneth certainly isn't the only one with a motive."

"Does that policeman know this?"

"No. I doubt it. But let's wait a while before we spread out all the family scandals for Farris."

"Why?"

"Because we don't know how serious Farris's arrest of Kenneth will be. Maybe we can handle this without turning Farris out after the rest of us."

Megan looked at me sharply.

"No," and I was answering the unspoken question, "I won't protect anyone else at Kenneth's expense. I promise you that."

"All right, K.C., but if it comes down to it, I'll tell the whole world everything I know if it will help Kenneth."

I understood that. I accepted it. And admired it.

"But what are we going to do right now?" she asked urgently. "Kenneth's in jail."

"Hire me. I'll go down there now. They can't refuse to let Kenneth see counsel. Later, if it comes to a trial, we can get somebody better than I am." I wasn't going on pride now. It might be Kenneth's life and there were criminal lawyers in town who could do more than I could. "If it comes to it, we'll get Jake Pinella. But, for right now, to get access to Kenneth, hire me."

TWELVE

A jail at one o'clock in the morning is a mournful place to be. The desk sergeant looked up from a copy of *True Detective* and watched me walk across the gritty concrete floor.

"You have a prisoner. Brought in about an hour ago. Kenneth Carlisle. I'm his lawyer and I want to see him."

The sergeant sighed. "Middle of the night, lady."

"You ever heard of the Miranda decision?"

"He's probably asleep."

"Wake him up."

Finally, he checked his booking records and called upstairs. He yanked his thumb toward the elevators.

"Third floor."

"Thanks."

The elevator smelled. I didn't try to figure out what it smelled like. I doubted that Kenneth had ever in his life visited the jail. Maybe as a young lawyer he had been appointed to defend an indigent. Knowing Kenneth, I would imagine he had managed to evade that unpleasant little duty. The elevator and the cops would be new to him. Of course, when your life is dissolving around you, I don't suppose it matters much whether the executioner wears a smile.

The elevator moved grudgingly upward. The door opened ponderously and I stepped out into the narrow corridor that faced the cage. Thick wire mesh separated me from the cage where the booking sergeant sat. Behind him was the heavy steel door that opened into the cellblock. To his right was a wooden door that I knew gave onto rooms where counsel could interview prisoners.

The booking sergeant was engrossed in a late-night flick. I knocked on the grillwork.

"Yeah?"

"I'm Kenneth Carlisle's lawyer."

"So?"

The late-night charm of the cops overwhelmed me.

"I want to see him."

"Jail opens at eight-thirty, a.m."

"That's great, but I want to see Carlisle now. If you don't bring him up, I'll get Judge Margolis on the phone."

Judge Margolis is a winter-faced ascetic with exceedingly strong views on the proper treatment of prisoners.

The sergeant worked the plug of tobacco in his mouth from one jaw to the other, spit a thick brown stream into a wastebasket, slowly stood, and came to the window.

"Lemme see your stuff."

I handed him my purse and briefcase. He pawed through them, shoved them back. "Come on."

He unlocked the door that opened into the cage, motioned me through, and relocked it. I followed him to the wooden door. He opened it, said, "Number three," and shut the door behind me.

I walked into number three and turned on the light. Two straight chairs sat on opposite sides of a rickety wooden table. An ashtray sat on the table. Barred windows, a spittoon and an old-fashioned silver-painted radiator completed the furnishings.

Kenneth came in and the door slammed behind him. He still wore his tuxedo. The bow tie was off and his shirt open at the throat. He looked disheveled, tired, and pale. He stood uncertainly just inside the door.

"I didn't call for you."

"I know, Kenneth. I heard you had been arrested and I went to your house. Megan hired me to represent you. She is frantic."

He winced. "Does she think—"

"She doesn't think you did it, Kenneth," I said quickly. "She is desperate to try and help you. That's why I'm here." Hurriedly, I added, "I'm not trying to . . . if it comes to a trial, Kenneth, we'll get Pinella. I know you would want the best."

Kenneth pushed a hand through his thick blond hair. "Trial? I hadn't even thought that far. They've been asking me questions, hundreds of questions."

"You haven't told them anything, have you?" I asked sharply. For God's sake, he was a lawyer. Surely he had kept his mouth shut.

"I haven't told them a damn thing. Not a damn thing," he said grimly. His face crinkled in an odd frown, "K.C.," he said simply, "I'm in a hell of a mess." He looked at me uncertainly. "Are you sure you want to get involved?" He paused, then added awkwardly, "You and I haven't . . . I mean, we went our separate ways a long time ago."

It was very quiet in the dingy little room, the quiet of late night, the quiet of isolation, the quiet of two people looking at each other, really looking, for the first time in years.

"I know." I looked at his tousled blond hair, at his weary face, and I didn't see the immaculate arrogant Kenneth I had seen for so many years. I saw a shocked and frightened man. My cousin. I remembered, achingly, the way he used to smile, when we were young, before we grew up and took on the masks of Kenneth Carlisle, establishment lawyer, and K.C. Carlisle, people's lawyer. I remembered his courtesy to Amanda and courtesy is just another form of love. I remembered the time he fought, grimly and not very well, an older heavier boy who was throwing rocks at the ducks on the lake one summer. Kenneth came out of it with a chipped front tooth and a black eye, not at all triumphant but utterly determined. I remembered the day he married Megan and the look in his eyes as he watched her walk down the aisle toward him.

"I don't think you killed anybody." I said it gruffly because I was trying not to cry.

"Thanks, K.C.," he said quietly. "I didn't. But nobody is going to believe me." He shook his head wearily. "Jesus Christ, I can't believe this is happening to me."

"Look, Kenneth, if we're going to get you out of this, I've got to know what's happened."

"Right."

We sat down at the wooden table. I lifted a yellow pad from my briefcase and laid it on the cigarette-burn-scarred surface.

"First . . . is Megan okay?"

"She's upset," I responded. It would do no good to tell Kenneth of the pain and shock in her eyes. "But Kenneth, she's sure you didn't do it."

"Did she say that?" His voice lifted and quickened and he looked years younger.

"Of course." I didn't remember her exact words. I don't know that she said it at all, but she didn't have to say it, it was implicit in her every word and gesture. And I needed Kenneth pepped up.

"Oh hey, that's great. I was afraid . . . I was afraid she might think . . ."

"She doesn't think you killed Francine, but, Kenneth, she knows something was wrong. She said it started about a month ago."

He rubbed his jaw. "Yeah."

"What was it, Kenneth? What did Francine know?"

"That bitch," he said softly.

That kind of talk wouldn't help him. It could make a bad situation worse, but he could say what he wanted to me and only to me. I was his lawyer and every word we exchanged was privileged.

"She wanted money?"

"Fifty thousand. I broke the trust to get it. I had to get the money without Megan knowing."

"You were going to pay up?"

"Yeah."

I could hear the prosecution now: *You were angry, weren't you, Mr. Carlisle? You were going to have to pay this woman fifty thousand dollars. That made you mad, didn't it, Mr. Carlisle? And even then you couldn't be sure your secret was safe. You decided there was a better way to keep her quiet, didn't you? You decided to make sure Francine Boutelle would never tell anyone . . .*

I shook my head, batting away the imagined diatribe. I knew the

DA, Jack Kerry. I knew his deep powerful voice. He would attack and batter a defendant, all within legal bounds, until a jury could scarcely hear another voice.

"What did Francine know, Kenneth?"

His hands, powerful hands, and it was odd that I had never noticed their size or strength before, gripped the edge of the table.

Powerful hands.

"You won't tell Megan?"

"Kenneth, for God's sake, whatever it is, we can't hide it forever. Believe me, Farris won't stop searching until he finds out."

He sagged tiredly in his chair. "If it all comes out, it's going to be hell for Megan."

It was already hell for Megan, but I didn't say that to Kenneth. It was odd, but apparently all that mattered to Kenneth was Megan and how his arrest affected her. He hadn't said a word about his political campaign. Had he even thought of it yet? Thought of the devastating impact his arrest would have upon the race? I really liked Kenneth even more. His total concern was for Megan.

And yet, a small whispery voice inside me wondered, was that all so wonderful? Wasn't this concern really just an extension of Kenneth's concern for himself because it was the loss of Megan's love that he feared? I felt caught in a welter of confusion. Was it his love for Megan or his love for himself that motivated him?

"I should have told Megan, told her years ago," Kenneth said dully. "But I thought it was so far behind me, not a part of our world."

It was not a pretty story, but it had happened a million times, would happen a million times more. A teenage girl, a teenage boy, first love and then, shockingly, an unwanted pregnancy. I remembered the girl, Christy Nelson. She was Kenneth's age, tall and willowy, a little silly, painfully middle class.

Grace must have been appalled.

Kenneth's bitter words echoed my thought, "Your mother was furious, of course. You know how important it is to her to be . . . socially impeccable." There was a world of disdain in his voice.

That was odd, too, because he and Megan were so definitely socially impeccable.

Grace said marriage was out of the question. My father agreed, though I would believe from a better motive.

"I can see now," he said painfully, "that it must have been pretty awful for Christy. Hell, we were just kids. The judge went to talk to her parents. He came back and told me that everything had been arranged, that Christy agreed that it was better that we not see each other again. Then they sent me off to Westover Academy to finish high school."

I remembered that. At the time, I had been puzzled, but what teenager really looks beyond himself? Kenneth went off to Westover, so what?

Abruptly, Kenneth slammed his hand against the table. "Goddamnit, I didn't know for years that she had the baby. I thought she was going to have an abortion. That's the only thing I really fault your dad about. He should have told me about the baby."

I suppose Mother and Dad thought they were handling it for the best, protecting everyone as well as they could. They set Christy up in an apartment in LA, paid her bills, put her through business college after the baby was born. Christy seemed not to have expected more.

"Christy was always easy to manage. She was cheerful, kind of silly, more interested in having a good time than in anything else."

He didn't know he was a father until Francine came to see him, six weeks earlier.

"I didn't believe it at first. I thought it was some kind of a put-up job. You know, the kind of thing that happens in political campaigns."

But Francine had the photocopy of the birth certificate. More tellingly, she had a picture of a ten-year-old girl named Kendra.

"I knew it was true," Kenneth said simply, "when I saw Kendra's picture."

Francine wanted $50,000, or a copy of the certificate and the picture would go to Megan.

"Why didn't you tell Megan immediately?" I asked. "It happened years ago, long before you knew Megan, why should Megan have cared at all?"

He looked at me unhappily. "Megan and I . . . a lot of people are jealous of us, you know. They think we have everything. That's how it looks to outsiders."

"Yes."

"But the one thing we don't have, can't have . . ."

"Yes?"

"Megan can't have children."

I didn't say anything for a long moment. Would it have mattered so much to Megan? Women are, after all, the ultimate realists. More than that, didn't Kenneth see that he would someday have to tell Megan, that blackmail once begun would never end?

"Kenneth, didn't you see that you would someday have to tell Megan? With someone like Francine, how could you trust her not to come back for more?"

My words trailed off. That would be the DA's question. *Are you trying to tell the jury, Mr. Carlisle, that you were so naive you thought you could pay off Miss Boutelle and forever buy her silence? Instead, didn't you decide to make sure she would never tell anyone?*

Kenneth wasn't listening to me. He was intent upon his own thoughts. "I had to pay Francine. I had to shut her up." His hands once again gripped the table, such big powerful hands. "I couldn't let Megan find out like that. To have a cheap bitch like Francine tell her, that would be the greatest insult of all."

I listened but I couldn't force my eyes away from Kenneth's hands. He looked down at them too and abruptly he let go of the table edge. Then he looked up at me. "What's wrong?"

"Nothing, nothing at all."

He knew. "It's all right," he said harshly, "you can relax. Francine wasn't strangled by hands."

I looked at him, appalled. How could he know that?

I must have stopped breathing for an instant.

"Jesus, K.C." he exclaimed, "don't look at me like that."

"But Kenneth," I asked huskily, "how do you know?"

"It's all right," he said wearily, "I was going to tell you. I know how she died. I was there."

"You were there when she was killed?"

"Oh God no, I didn't mean that. No. I found her dead."

It had happened much as with me but with several differences. Critical differences. Differences that could convict Kenneth of murder.

"I was supposed to bring the fifty thousand at seven o'clock. I left the office around six-thirty, I was too restless to sit there and wait. I drove around, down to the beach, then, finally, over to Francine's apartment. I got there a little early. About five to seven."

His ring had not been answered or his knock. Kenneth almost said to hell with it, almost went home.

"But I kept thinking, she's probably just gone to run an errand. If I don't give her the money, she'll call Megan. I knocked again, hard and gave the knob a little twist. The door opened and I decided to go in and wait for her."

So he found her.

"It was . . . sickening. I kept staring at her face. It was awful."

I knew that. I had seen her, too, her face blotched and swollen, the tongue protruding.

"I looked down," and there was growing horror in his voice, "I looked at her throat and I could see how she was strangled and I couldn't believe it. I thought I was losing my mind."

I waited and I could swear his horror was genuine.

"She was strangled with my scarf. With the white silk scarf Megan gave me for Christmas last year."

"Oh Kenneth . . ."

I started to say that was impossible but I knew from his face that it was true.

"Are you sure?" I asked.

He nodded heavily. "It was custom made. My initials are in the lower right hand corner in gold thread. I know it's crazy, but it's true. It's my scarf and I swear to God that I didn't kill her."

I stared at him in growing shock for there had been no scarf when I found her.

"Kenneth, oh my God, did you take the scarf?"

"Yes."

I had a sudden dreadful picture of Kenneth bending over that inert sprawled body, desperately working on the soft silk, trying to get it loose from that swollen neck. It was his breathing, frantic with haste and fear, we heard on the recorder.

"Oh Kenneth, you shouldn't have done that." Because I could see no way that anyone, Farris or a jury, would ever believe Kenneth was innocent.

"I know. But if I'd left it . . . hell, there wasn't any way anybody would believe me then, either. I couldn't leave it there. I was sure it would convict me. I kept trying to get it off and it was awful. My hands kept touching her skin and she was still warm. I thought I was going to be sick. I had to yank it finally . . . and her hair shook . . ."

But taking the scarf hadn't helped him. It had made it worse.

"Ferris found the scarf in your trunk?"

"Yeah."

I stared at Kenneth.

"I didn't do it. I know it looks bad, but I didn't do it."

It didn't look bad. It looked impossible. How had that scarf come into the possession of the murderer?

"Had you ever been to her apartment before?"

"Never."

"Had she ever come to your office?"

"Yes, but just once. That first visit, about six weeks ago." He shook his head. "That won't help. I had the scarf Monday."

On Monday and this was Wednesday night. No, actually now it was early Thursday morning.

Kenneth frowned in concentration. "That's the last day I remember seeing it. It was foggy Monday morning. Megan got my all-weather coat out of the closet and pulled the scarf down from a hook."

He had had a touch of a sore throat. Megan had looped the scarf around his neck, tucked it inside his coat. To keep him warm. "You have a lot of speeches to make, Kenneth. You can't afford to get sick." He had laughed. He'd no intention of getting sick. The campaign was taking shape and he felt confident now he could beat Greg Garrison. He didn't need the scarf but he took it because Megan wanted him to.

"Monday was the last day you wore it?"

Kenneth nodded.

Monday. That was the day we met at Kenneth's office to dissolve the Cochran-Carlisle trust and at Grace's that evening to discuss how we could face down Francine Boutelle.

It was cold in that dingy, ill-lighted room on the third floor of the La Luz County Jail, but the chill of the room didn't account for the icy tingle in my mind.

Kenneth and I both understood the implication.

"When did you miss it on Monday?"

"I wore it to the office. I didn't go out for lunch because I was too busy getting ready for the meeting. I had a sandwich at my desk. That evening, Megan met me at the office and we drove to Grace's. I know I didn't wear it, but it could have been in my coat pocket. I usually fold it and stuff it in my coat pocket. It was fairly warm when we left the office so I didn't think of it. That night, when we started home from your mother's, there was a cold breeze. I remember standing in the foyer and reaching into the pocket of my coat. It wasn't there. I was kind of surprised but I thought it must have dropped out onto the floor of the coat closet at the office. I didn't think of it again. Until tonight."

The scarf could have been taken from Kenneth's coat pocket by anyone at his office or by anyone at Grace's. That number included, of course, quite a few people with no love for Francine Boutelle.

The scarf made all the difference. To Chief Farris, it proved Kenneth's guilt. To me, it suggested that someone had decided in advance to kill Francine. Someone who thought ahead. Someone with very little regard for Kenneth.

I could have taken the scarf. So could Travis or Edmond, Priscilla or Grace. So could Edmond's wife, Sue, or Travis' wife, Lorraine.

A white silk scarf. The unnecessary accoutrement of a rich man. A white silk circle around the Carlisle family.

THIRTEEN

I should have expected it, but the circus atmosphere in the corridor outside the courtroom next morning caught me by surprise. TV and still cameramen jostled for the best shot. Local, state, and wire reporters surrounded Kenneth and me and Kenneth's police escort when we stepped off the elevator on our way to the arraignment.

"Hey, Carlisle, look this way."

"C'mon, man, hold your head up, that's a way."

"Did you kill her, Carlisle?"

"What's the word on the race, Carlisle? Will you be stepping down as the nominee?"

"Hey, Carlisle, was Boutelle your girlfriend? What's the story, man?"

For a man accustomed to deference, it must have been difficult. Kenneth stopped at the doorway to the courtroom and held up his hand. In an instant it was quiet, the portable mikes held up.

"I intend to plead not guilty. If I am released on bail, I will hold a news conference this afternoon. If I am denied bail, I will release a statement through my attorney."

Then he pushed on into the courtroom.

For a man with his back to the wall, it wasn't a bad effort. I was busy thinking about the promised statement as we walked to the defense table. I had drafted a lot of documents in my five years of practice, but I didn't have any idea how to draft a statement to the press.

Judge Foley drew the arraignment. He was an old friend of Dad's but he looked down at us with no change of expression when I stood to speak for the defendant. I really didn't know what to expect. Sometimes a murder defendant is released on bail. It depends a lot upon the judge, the defendant and the circumstances of the crime. Nobody is going to let loose an axe murderer or sex deviate. On the other hand, if the defendant is a stable member of the community and isn't considered a danger to the public, bail will be set.

Judge Foley accepted the charge, received Kenneth's plea of not guilty, listened to the assistant DA's request for a half-million dollar bond. I immediately requested a reduction. Judge Foley impassively studied the notes he had made then, brusquely, set bail at $100,000 and bound Kenneth over for trial on the next docket. I had already made arrangements with a bail bondsman should bail be granted.

On the way out of the courtroom, the reporters surrounded us and it was bedlam again. I felt an instant of panic, then a strong hand gripped my elbow.

"This way, K.C. I have a car waiting downstairs."

Harry Nichols shouldered us through the crowd.

An angry reporter yelled, "Hey, Nichols, what do you think you're doing? Setting up some kind of exclusive for *The Beacon?* Carlisle will regret it if..."

"You've got your story for now," Nichols replied brusquely. "The same story I've got. Carlisle's pleaded not guilty and he'll hold a news conference this afternoon."

I realized that Harry must have been near at hand during the turmoil when Kenneth spoke out before we entered the courtroom. Now Harry held the reporters and photographers at bay while we hurried into the small private elevator used by the judges. It was only a moment's respite, though. Some of the harder and leaner media types were waiting for us at ground level, but Harry knew how to handle them.

"Four o'clock, folks. At Carlisle's office."

A black Mercedes with a chauffeur waited, motor running. Harry opened the front door for Kenneth, and he and I slid into the back seat.

As the car pulled away, Kenneth looked back at us, bewildered.

"You're Harry Nichols, aren't you?" Kenneth asked.

"Right."

Kenneth looked wary and totally puzzled. "You've always gone out of your way to fight me."

Harry nodded, his face forbidding. "Right. I may do so in the future. But I've done some checking, Mr. Carlisle, on Francine Boutelle. She worked for an LA paper at one time. She was fired because she tried to get money for not running a story. I don't like that. I like a lot less the idea that she was setting up *The Beacon* with her letter to me. Nobody determines what *The Beacon* will run except me." Harry looked at me. "I've seen the way your cousin has come to your defense. I don't know whether you are guilty or innocent, but I like loyalty." Harry smiled and he looked years younger and quite charming. "Besides, if this all washes out and you're exonerated, *The Beacon* will probably profit from an exclusive interview."

Kenneth managed a slight smile at that. "Believe me, I'll be glad to give you one, under those circumstances." He looked out of the front window. "Where are we going?"

"I've asked Ed to take us to your house. Is that all right?" Nichols asked.

"Yes," Kenneth said wearily. "Yes. I'd like to go home."

When we reached Kenneth's drive and pulled into it, the front door opened. Megan stood on the steps, waiting.

Kenneth opened the door and was out before the car stopped. Then he stopped and looked up toward Megan.

"Kenneth," she cried, "oh Kenneth," and she ran down the steps and into his arms.

"Go on," Harry told the chauffeur and the Mercedes glided quietly out of the drive.

We sat back against the soft comfortable upholstery. I was suddenly tired, so tired.

"Poor devil," Harry said abruptly.

The tone of pity in his voice frightened me.

Harry looked at me soberly. "He hasn't got a chance, K.C."

"Why do you say that?"

"Farris has some solid evidence. I don't know what it is, but the rumor is out that it's solid gold."

The scarf, of course.

"I know what it is."

I told him and suddenly the pity in his eyes was for me. "Jesus, K.C."

"He didn't do it. I don't care how it looks, Harry. To me that scarf proves the crime was premeditated." I told him when Kenneth had last seen the scarf and who could have had access to it.

I could tell that Harry thought I was grasping at straws.

"I'm afraid the scarf can't be explained away, but you could be right. You could be. Anyway, I've picked up some information that might be helpful to you. I thought we might stop for lunch at El Pajarito and I'll tell you what I've found out."

El Pajarito is on the outskirts of La Luz and overlooks the sea. It sounded very appealing, the quiet and elegance, and the distance from the pressures that would push at me once I went back to my office.

"I'd like that."

It was early and we had the terrace overlooking the water to ourselves. We had a very private table with a vine-covered trellis between us and the other tables. The sweet scent of the vines mingled with the damp sea air.

"I noticed that the maitre d' led us here without a question. Do you come often?"

"This is my table. It's always held for me."

He said it matter-of-factly, sure of himself and his place in the world.

The waiter hovered near by and we made our choices quickly, ordering beer and the specialty of the day, red snapper *a la veracruz.*

The beer came in icy bottles beaded with water. I took a deep drink, savored the light, slightly acrid taste.

"I've been on the phone, finding out what I could. For starters, the cops are sure Carlisle's the killer. The investigation is over except for what they can pile up against him."

The brisk breeze off the sea rustled the vines behind us. It was a lonely sound, as lonely as the dull roar of breakers. I looked at Harry in dismay. He was telling me there wasn't any hope for Kenneth, that it was cut-and-dried so far as the police were concerned.

If Kenneth were innocent, no one was doing anything about it.

Francine's killer was home free.

Unless I could find him.

The only way I could find him was through Francine. I pulled my legal pad out of my briefcase.

"Okay, Harry," I said grimly, "what have you got?"

Much of it was repetitive, the same personal history of Francine that Pamela Reeves had produced. He did have one interesting fact. Francine worked at the Cocoa Butter from the time she was fired from the LA paper until she came to La Luz. So she had given up her night club job to write the article on the Carlisles.

"I called Fred Sheltie, the managing editor of *Inside Out,*" Harry explained. "She showed up in his office about seven weeks ago and said she had a great idea for a story on a very well-known California family. Of course, the Carlisles aren't in a class with the Hearsts or Chandlers, but they are well enough known for the idea to interest Fred. She told him just enough so that he thought it had real possibilities, especially since Kenneth was running for Congress. He told her she could submit it on a freelance basis."

It was clear Francine had zeroed in on the Carlisles on her own hook, not at the instigation of the magazine. It suggested some kind of contact with the family, or, at the least, someone who knew a great deal about us.

The waiter brought our plates then, steam rising from the fish with its thin red sauce. I peppered my salad and wondered whether Pamela had done any more looking for me. I needed a clearer picture of Francine's circle of acquaintances. Somewhere among the people she knew must be a link to the Carlisles.

I realized then that Harry was still talking and I hadn't heard a word of it.

"Sorry. What did you say?"

"I just said it was odd, but the police so far hadn't found any trace of a story on the Carlisles in her papers or tapes."

I laid my fork down and stared at Harry. "Nothing on the family? Nothing at all?"

"Just a list of the Carlisles she intended to interview. All of the names had check marks by them."

Oh yes, she had talked to all of us, she had indeed.

The room where she died had shown evidences of search. Was that what had been taken, the manuscript?

I suppose my relief was evident.

Harry's cool grey eyes narrowed. "So that was the game. She was up to her old tricks?"

I hesitated, but, hell, it was obvious if he thought about it.

"Yes. She was offering not to print her most interesting tidbits—for a price."

"How much?"

"Fifty thousand. From each of us."

"That could add up to a nice sum."

I had never totaled it, but Harry was right. If all of us had been willing to pay her off, she would have scored big. I added it up in my mind, me, Kenneth, Priscilla, Edmond, Travis, and Grace. Three hundred thousand dollars. Not bad pay for a beginner.

"If Farris finds out about the story, it will pretty well close the gate on your cousin."

I suppose my alarm must have shown.

Harry reached across the table, took my hand. "Don't look like that. If I'm asked, I don't know a damn thing—except what I read in the newspapers."

His hand was warm and strong, a link to a saner world, but a reminder too that I didn't now belong in that world, the world where the police could be counted on to look for killers. I was committed to hiding ugly facts and twisting and turning to try and find a way out of danger for Kenneth.

I felt suddenly very tired and very alone.

"What are you going to do, K.C.? Hire a private detective?"

"I'm not sure, Harry." I told him about John Solomon and Pamela. "The most important thing is to find out who might have taken Kenneth's scarf."

The possibilities were terribly limited. All those who had access to it had motives. That was the hell of it. They all had motives and they were all Carlisles.

"From Carlisle's office or from your mother's house, is that right?" Harry asked.

I nodded.

Harry understood my dilemma.

If I set out to seek Francine's murderer to save Kenneth, I might substitute one kin for another in the prisoner's dock.

"I'm sorry," he said quietly.

After lunch, the chauffeur drove us to my office. As I got out of the car, Harry said, "Be careful."

"I will, Harry."

"I'll call you soon."

"Please do." I meant it.

I liked him although I don't suppose many people would find him likable. He was aloof and self-assured, certain always to follow his own inclinations. I understood that. I was thinking of the kindness he had shown me, the help he had offered me, despite the estrangement of our families. I was tired and worried but smiling, and totally unprepared for what awaited me in my office.

Greg was standing just inside the door and he was furious.

"Who the hell was that?" He grabbed my arm.

Pat took one look and slowly rose from behind his desk. He looked at me questioningly.

"It's all right, Pat," I said quickly. "You're hurting my arm, Greg."

Greg dropped my arm but stood, pugnacious and scowling, looming over me.

"Greg, for heaven's sake, what's the matter with you?"

"Who's your friend in the chauffeur-driven limousine?"

"He is not exactly a friend."

"Oh, more than that?"

"It's Harry Nichols. The owner of *The Beacon*" I didn't like standing in my office foyer, explaining myself. "Come on in my office," I said impatiently.

I shut the office door behind us and walked on to my desk. Greg stood just inside the door, anger clear in the taut line of his body.

"When did you start running around with him?"

I dropped into my chair. "I don't," I said coolly "run around with anybody, Greg. If you read the newspapers, you might know that Nichols and I happened on Francine's body at almost the same time last night."

Greg stared at me. "You didn't call last night. I waited and waited. You find a body and you don't even call me. Were you out with him?"

There was no question who Greg meant.

"As a matter of fact, yes. He offered to buy me a drink after the police let us go. I accepted."

"You should have called me," he repeated stubbornly. "You didn't call this morning. I canceled a campaign trip. I came here. I called your apartment. I went down to the courthouse but I missed you."

"I'm sorry," I said contritely. "But everything's happened so quickly. I had to help Kenneth. I went to his house after he was arrested last night, then to the jail. I represented him at the arraignment this morning."

"What were you doing with Nichols again this morning?"

"He's offered to help me. He had found out some things about Francine and he wanted to tell me."

"I'm the one who can help you," Greg said quickly. "I know a hell of a lot more about these things than Nichols."

Greg was right there. He had been DA before Jack Kerry. Greg had prosecuted a dozen murder trials.

"I know, Greg. And I'm counting on you. You know that."

The hard tight lines around Greg's mouth eased. "Hell, K.C., I'm sorry," he said gruffly. "I didn't mean to lose my temper, but I was just about to go crazy with worry over you. Last night, I was worried sick. You didn't call and didn't call. I rang your apartment. I even went by but you weren't there. I didn't know what to think."

I had probably just missed Greg. I got back to my apartment about three a.m. and collapsed into an uneasy sleep for a few hours before I was up and arranging bond, should it be approved, and planning for the arraignment.

"This morning," Greg continued, "when I saw all this stuff in the papers, I couldn't believe you hadn't called me.

He came to me, pulled me up out of my chair and held me hard against him. "Jesus, K.C., you should have called."

Abruptly, he kissed me, his mouth hard and demanding against mine. The fatigue that dulled my mind and body burned away and I was, suddenly, kissing him in return and there was a wild surge of excitement between us. Then, in an ugly twist of memory, I could hear Grace's voice, "Perhaps we could buy you a stud farm," and I was abruptly as limp and cold as seaweed left behind by the outgoing tide.

"K.C.?"

I gave his arm a quick squeeze and slipped out of his embrace. I brushed my hair from my face. "I'm sorry, Greg, I'm very tired." I was tired. I had slept perhaps four hours after finally getting home from the jail. The arraignment and the crush of reporters had taken a further toll. I ached with fatigue.

"K.C.," he said gruffly, "I didn't mean to make things harder. It's just that you mean so much to me."

For the first time since I had known Greg, I felt that I was hearing him speak without any pretense. There was always so much ebullience in him. Now he spoke quietly, opening himself to me.

I looked into his eyes, dark commanding eyes now strangely uncertain. I almost told him that I cared, too. Yet, damn Grace, was it caring or passion with me? Greg was incredibly exciting.

I hesitated and the moment was gone.

I did say quickly, too quickly, after that long silence, "I wish we could go somewhere, the two of us, get out of all of this."

Now he hesitated. That was impossible. For both of us.

"Yeah," he said heavily. "That would be nice, but . . ." Then he said awkwardly, "Well, look, K.C., I'm sorry about your cousin. I hope . . . I hope everything works out."

"Thank you, Greg."

He frowned. "Don't take it wrong, K.C. I know you're a damn good lawyer, but I believe, if I were you, I'd get Pinella."

I nodded. "If it comes to a trial, Greg, that's what we'll do."

"If it comes to a trial?" he repeated.

"Yes. You see, Greg, Kenneth is innocent. I'm sure of it. I'm going to be working on it, finding out more about Francine."

He wished me luck before he left and we talked about getting together later in the week, except he had some heavy campaigning to do. It was a little stilted and I felt let down after he left. Then I shrugged it away. Greg and I could patch it up, I was sure of it, and, right now, Kenneth needed my thoughts.

FOURTEEN

I told Pat to hold my calls and remake all appointments for next week. I settled down to work.

In an hour, I had it laid out—and it looked bad for the Carlisles.

Item: Boutelle came to La Luz to write the Carlisle story.

Item: To our knowledge, Boutelle had no other contacts in La Luz.

Item: She was strangled with Kenneth's silk scarf.

That, of course, was the whammy.

If her head had been smashed by a poker, we could reasonably imagine her attacker to be anyone, a maniac stranger who happened to pick her as a victim, a neighbor irritated by her cat, a door-to-door salesman overcome by the lust to kill, a devil-ridden evangelist with homicidal tendencies.

It was impossible that any of the above could have come into possession of Kenneth's scarf.

What did we know about the scarf?

Item: Kenneth wore it to work Monday. He did not think of it again until leaving Grace's house Monday evening. When he reached into his pocket, the scarf was gone.

Conclusion: The scarf could have been taken by anyone at Kenneth's office or by anyone at Grace's house that evening. The latter included me, Priscilla, Grace, Edmond and Sue, and Travis and Lorraine.

I read my notes and reread them. So far as I could figure, there was only one possible killer other than a Carlisle. And he was a very slender possibility, indeed, because I could imagine no way that he could have obtained the scarf. But I decided to start my search with him. I would turn back into the family only when that was my only recourse.

I leaned back in my chair. I must remember exactly what Francine had said, that night we talked.

I had been tired then, too, tired from the long drive home from Rosemont and it had taken me a little while to realize that Francine Boutelle wasn't an investigative reporter. She had begun by talking about the Levy case, claiming Dad had accepted a bribe. She pointed to Albert Gersten, Sonia Levy's nephew, as the bagman. I concentrated furiously. Boutelle got her information from Gersten's ex-wife. What was her name? Veronica? No. Victoria? No. Natalie. That was it, Natalie Gersten.

I found Natalie Gersten in her redwood hot tub behind her split-level house on Ruidoso Canyon Drive. As the maid showed me to the flagstone patio beside the hot tub, Mrs. Gersten, her hair covered by a silk turban, was studying my card. All that showed above the redwood circle was the turban and a bony hand holding the card.

"Come around here, darling, where I can see you."

She was flushed from the heat of the water and perhaps from the red wine in a glass that was set upon a ledge. She had once been beautiful as a glossy raven is beautiful but now her face was haggard and, more than that, bitter. You could read it in the sharp deep lines that bracketed her mouth and in the purse of her lips.

"K.C. Carlisle?"

I nodded.

She glanced back down at my card. On it I had penciled, 'May I see you on a matter of importance?'

It would take monumental indifference to ignore that request, or extreme caution. Most women possess neither.

She looked up sharply. "If you're here from my ex-husband, I don't have a damn thing to say."

"I have nothing to do with your husband, Mrs. Gersten."

"Ex-husband."

Here must be the source of those lines of bitterness. It wouldn't take much to loose a torrent. I chose my words carefully.

"At least," I amended, "I am not here on his behalf. I do have a question about some activity of his in the past." I paused and added delicately, "Perhaps it could even be described as a criminal activity."

It is, of course, as much a crime to bribe as to be bribed.

She listened avidly and there was a dart of pleasure in her dark eyes.

"I could tell you where the bones are buried," she said meaningfully, "if I wanted to." She hungered to. She propped her arms along the side of the tub and hot water bubbled and swirled around her bony shoulders.

I felt a surge of disgust. What was I doing here, baiting a vindictive middle-aged woman to destroy my father's memory? But I managed an approving smile, though it felt grotesque. I wouldn't think of Dad now. I would think of Kenneth.

"Do you remember when your husband's uncle, Adolphus Levy—"

"Ex-husband."

"Yes, of course. When your ex-husband's uncle was tried for fraud. My father, Judge Carlisle, heard the case."

"Sure, and cleaned up fifty thousand to let old Adolphus off the hook. Sure, I remember. Albert took care of it." She laughed and it was a hard ugly sound in the soft California air. "Albert was always such a goody-goody. He didn't want to have anything to do with it but his Aunt Sonia could always pull his string. Poor Albert. He writhed and wriggled and whined but he finally took the money and delivered it. Sonia made him do it. He said it was wrong and just plain highway robbery, that old Adolphus was innocent and shouldn't have to buy his way out, but Sonia wasn't going to take any chances. There isn't anything she wouldn't do for that old dried-up string she's married to. She's the one who set it up. She's a hard old bitch."

That was all she knew. It was enough to make me feel physically ill. I refused a glass of wine, thanked her—God, how could I thank her—and made my escape.

As I drove down the twisting canyon road, I knew how Pandora must have felt. I had pursued this clue because it led away from Kenneth, but I was breaking my heart.

I believed in my father. I believed in him. I remembered how fairly he treated everyone in his court, lawyers, jurors, plaintiffs, defendants. Always.

He wasn't a greedy man, although sometimes he must have been a little hard pressed since the great bulk of the family fortune skipped his generation, but I never remembered an instance of his talking about a great need for money or indeed evidencing any kind of interest in money at all.

Yet I now had heard, albeit second-hand from a hate-filled woman, a clear unambiguous claim that he had accepted a bribe.

I tried not to think of it, tried not to picture my father taking money to suspend a sentence. I tried instead to think, should the tawdry story be true, of the panic on the part of the man who paid the money when it looked like the story might be made public. Albert Gersten was an investment banker. He would not like to go to jail.

I pushed away the memory of the day I was graduated from law school and my father reached out to shake my hand and say quietly, with so much pride, "You will be the finest kind of lawyer, K.C."

No man who admired the law, loved the law, could sell justice for money.

At the base of the canyon where the streets widen out and a new sub-development crowds against the hills, I stopped at a convenience store and went to an outside pay phone. I looked up the Levys' number.

"Who is calling?" the maid asked.

"K.C. Carlisle. Please tell Mrs. Levy that it is very important that I speak to her."

Sonia Levy's voice was cool and placid. "Hello."

"Mrs. Levy, we've never met, but I think you knew my father, Judge Carlisle."

There was a distinct pause.

"No, Miss Carlisle," she said finally. "I did not know your father personally. My only acquaintance with him came when my husband Adolphus was tried in his court. And exonerated."

The last was sharp and pointed. The wound still throbbed.

"Mrs. Levy, I must talk to you personally."

"Why?"

"I have heard a charge that your nephew, Albert Gersten, bribed my father to suspend Mr. Levy's sentence."

"That is an absurd accusation, Miss Carlisle. I would ignore it if I were you."

"You don't understand, Mrs. Levy. A murder is involved."

"Murder?"

"Yes."

"What are you talking about, Miss Carlisle? Please explain yourself."

"I will be glad to do so. In person."

"I'm sorry. Miss Carlisle. I see no reason why . . ."

"Then I suppose I must talk to Albert Gersten."

There was a long silence.

"That shouldn't be necessary," she said finally. "When would you like to meet?"

"Now."

"Very well."

The Levy house was on the opposite side of La Luz, a beachfront home. Prices on these have been out of sight for years. Only Saudi sheiks need now apply. I drove slowly. I had a lot to think about. It was clear that Sonia Levy did not want me to talk to Albert Gersten. That suggested Albert might be a weak reed. If I didn't get anywhere with Mrs. Levy, I would try him next.

The brief enigmatic phone conversation had done nothing to relieve the depression that dragged me down. If my father turned out to be a crook, it meant nothing could ever be what it seemed. I had scarcely trusted anyone since my sister maneuvered a sailboat away from me, willing me to drown. If my father was not what he seemed, I would never again have faith in the faces that people turned toward me.

The Levy mansion of grey stone clung to the cliff top. It spelled a lot of money, money enough to buy whatever Sonia Levy wanted.

She waited for me in her library. Silver and blue Persian rugs graced the highly-waxed oak floor. Books rose in tiers on mahogany shelving. She was standing at the far end of the room, beneath an oil portrait. I glanced up at it and was caught by the vividness of the portrait. It was of a man in his fifties with thinning grey hair and a slight build but the painter had captured in the face a suggestion of kindness and sensitivity that was striking.

"Do you admire it, Miss Carlisle?"

"Yes."

"That is my husband. Miss Carlisle. Can you not look at his face and see the kind of man he is?"

I nodded.

"Everyone knows how good Adolphus is," she continued heatedly. "Everyone. It was an abomination that he should have been persecuted as he was. It broke his heart. He has never recovered from it." She spoke angrily. The passage of years had not, for her, eased the pain of his arrest and trial.

"The sentence was suspended."

She lifted her chin. She was an elegant woman, her blue-grey hair coiffed perfectly, her makeup subtle and flattering. Slim and tall, she wore her ultra-suede dress with the flair of a wealthy woman who knows and loves clothes. Her dark eyes, rich brown eyes, looked at me dispassionately. "Yes," she agreed without expression, "the sentence was suspended."

Painfully, I said, "I have heard the charge that my father accepted money to suspend the sentence. Is that true?"

Sonia Levy clasped her hands in front of her. They were lovely hands, slim and dark, and she wore gracefully a heavy silver bracelet and one ring with a blood-red ruby stone that glowed even in the subdued light of the library.

"I want to know, Miss Carlisle, what you meant when you spoke of murder?"

"It was in the papers this morning. A woman was strangled here in La Luz. Francine Boutelle."

"I do not know the name. What could she have to do with us?"

"She was writing an article about the Carlisle family for *Inside Out.* In it she planned to say that Albert Gersten bribed my father. At your direction."

"Are you suggesting," she said it slowly, thoughtfully, "that Albert or I could have killed this woman to keep the matter secret?"

I hadn't envisioned Sonia Levy as a murderess, but, logically, it could be.

"Yes," I said simply.

She turned away from me, walked to a rosewood table next to a sofa and picked up the morning paper. She returned to me, all the while skimming the article.

She read aloud, "Miss Boutelle was known to have been alive at six p.m. because she telephoned to a neighborhood delicatessen to order some food. There was no answer at her door when the delicatessen attempted delivery at about seven-thirty. Her body was discovered shortly before eight o'clock by La Luz attorney K.C. Carlisle, cousin of the man charged with her murder." Mrs. Levy looked up at me with dark measuring eyes. "You found the body."

I nodded.

Abruptly, she began to smile and the atmosphere of the room eased. "I am delighted to be able to inform you, Miss Carlisle, that my husband and I, and my nephew, Albert Gersten, left La Luz in the company of another couple, Paul and Camille Richards, at shortly before six p.m. on our way to attend a party in Los Angeles at the home of Harris Porter. We arrived there at seven-thirty and did not leave until almost midnight."

I recognized the name. Porter had directed pictures which won back-to-back Oscars.

As an alibi, it was impeccable.

So Albert and Mrs. Levy were out of it. It didn't really surprise me. And it didn't ease my pain.

"All right, Mrs. Levy, I accept that. But please, I must know the truth. About my father."

She looked around the room. She paused, then asked gently, "Miss Carlisle, have you ever seen my roses? They are quite lovely. Even this late in the season."

I followed her through the French windows of the library onto a sloping terrace. Roses, glorious beds of roses, cascaded toward the cliffs edge. As we walked toward the center of the garden, she reached out and touched me gently on my arm. "Why do you not let it go, Miss Carlisle? There can be no joy in disturbing the dead."

"I must know."

She looked out toward the sea. It was metallic today, reflecting the heavy grey clouds that scudded restlessly overhead.

"I did not know your father," she began, "but, during the trial, I came to feel he was a good man, a kind man. A man much like my Augustus. In my heart, I began to sing for I thought that one such man would know another."

She reached out, lightly touched a yellow rose.

"Every fall, I hold open house for the La Luz Rose Club. I do not belong to the club, you understand, but always they want to see my roses and I invite them. I went ahead with the open house that fall, the year Adolphus was tried, because I did not want anyone to think I was . . . ashamed. An innocent man has no need to hide, or his family, Miss Carlisle. I held the open house. It was the last week of the trial. After I had guided everyone about, shown them my beds, I urged them all to enjoy the tea which I had arranged on tables on the terrace. There was a woman who seemed to stay near me, all that afternoon. Finally, as everyone began to move toward the terrace, she came up to me and asked if she could speak to me privately for a moment. I was surprised, but of course I said yes. I was the hostess."

She pointed to the cliffs edge about forty yards away.

"There, do you see the wooden railing?"

I nodded.

"We walked to it and went down the steps and stood, all by ourselves, on a platform we have built there, just above the sea."

At first there was an awkward silence, but then the woman spoke hurriedly, scarcely above a whisper, to Sonia Levy.

"She asked if I wanted to be certain my husband would be freed. I was so surprised. I said, of course, I should like that. She was very pale and she kept looking up at the cliff to be sure no one stood near. Then she said she could arrange it. For a sum."

I was bewildered. None of this made any sense. None of it seemed possible.

"Who was she?" I asked. "Surely you demanded to know who she was?"

Mrs. Levy looked at me sadly. "Oh yes, of course I did that. I was not a downy duck." She paused, "I am sorry, Miss Carlisle. I did not want to tell you but you have insisted."

"Who was she?" I asked steadily.

"Your mother. Miss Carlisle."

"I see," I said slowly. I did see. I saw a great many things.

Sonia Levy walked with me to my car. As we said goodbye, she was kind. She tried to be helpful. "Remember, Miss Carlisle, we cannot always judge others."

I thanked her. I knew that she meant I should not be disappointed in my father. But, as I drove away, I wasn't thinking about Dad.

I was thinking only of Grace.

The shadows were lengthening as I drove home. No. Not home. Grace's house. I gave no thought to time or to who might be there. When I swung into the long circular drive, I saw Chinese lanterns strung in the trees and two servants lounging on the garden seats just past the front door. They stubbed out their cigarettes and sprang to attention as my Porsche skidded to a stop at the base of the front steps.

I was out of the car before one of them hurried up. "May I park your car, Miss?"

"Don't bother."

He looked uncomfortable. "Please, miss, if you block the front drive, we won't be able to park all the cars."

"What is it? A party?"

The second man had arrived now. He overheard me and said officiously, "By invitation only, Miss. If you . . ."

"I'm part of the family," I said brusquely, over my shoulder, and started up the steps.

Anger swept me ahead, a swirling wave of anger. A party. Amanda dead two days and a party. The funeral was in the morning. Amanda dead and my father's honor destroyed, but Grace was giving a party.

I opened the front door, startling a maid who was putting fresh water in the vases along the hallway.

"Where is Mrs. Carlisle?"

"Upstairs, Miss. May I ask . . ."

Of course Grace would be upstairs. Dressing for a party was a ritual with her, as much to be treasured as the moment when the guests arrived to find her standing, serene and regal, in her drawing room. First came the long luxurious bath with the creamy oil of gardenia swirling in the soft water. Then a rest in her silk negligee on the satiny chaise-lounge in the alcove of her dressing room. Finally, a half-hour before the guests were to arrive, the slow and careful application of her makeup and the donning of her dress. A blue dress, usually. Blue is so becoming for blondes. Even aging blondes.

I burst into her room.

I was right on target. She was standing in front of her full-length mirror, admiring her image, the soft crushed silk dress, the string of perfect pearls. She swung about, one hand at her throat. "K.C., you startled me. When will you learn not to slam and bang about?"

I wasn't ten years old to be quailed or fifteen to be snubbed. I stood just inside the door and stared at her.

No one ever said Grace wasn't perceptive.

"K.C., what's wrong?"

"I just talked to Sonia Levy."

She took a quick breath. She clutched her throat as if breath were, suddenly, impossible to find.

I knew it was true.

Grace didn't say a word. She stood there, looking old and sick and grey.

"What did you need the money for, Grace?" My voice shook with anger. "What in the hell did you need the money for?"

She turned and walked blindly toward her dressing table and slumped into the chair. She leaned forward, hiding her face in her hands.

I crossed the room, stood beside her. "It was easy, wasn't it?" I asked bitterly. "So easy."

She made no answer, would not look up.

"It won't do any good to hide, Grace. I know how you did it. Dad talked about his cases to you. Judges aren't supposed to, of course, but it helped him make up his mind, a kind of thinking out loud. It never occurred to him that you would ever divulge anything you heard. He didn't worry about you. For one thing, I suppose in his heart he knew you usually didn't listen. You didn't care. You didn't care how he thought, how he worked. But he should have worried about you, shouldn't he?"

Her hands dropped. She raised a ravaged face. "Please, K.C."

"No, Grace. I won't stop. Not this time. Not until I know how it happened."

Her mouth worked. Finally, faintly, she asked, "That Levy woman. What is she going to do?"

That was Grace, of course. Always concerned about Grace. Always.

"Listen to me," I said harshly, "you are going to tell me the truth. This one time you are going to tell the truth. Why did you do it?"

Her fingers began to pleat the soft silk of her dress. "I had to do it, K.C., I had to. If I didn't pay, he was going to tell your father."

"He?"

Her fingers moved harder, faster. "Larry. Larry Stephenson."

"What did he threaten to tell Dad?"

She shook her head, back and forth. "I didn't mean . . . I had no idea that he . . ." She stopped.

"Go on, Grace."

"He was so kind at first. So sweet and . . . and loving. I never intended anything to happen. But that day he went with me, to the lake house . . . and then, it was so exciting. But I never meant for it to go so far."

"You had an affair with him?"

"K.C."

So it was not to be mentioned directly. That was too shocking, too insensitive. Crude K.C. would spell it out.

I could have shaken her until her perfectly arranged hair collapsed into an untidy mess. I could have . . . Suddenly, I was tired. Because of her incredibly benighted views of sex, she had bartered away my father's integrity.

"K.C.," and she was pleading, "I had to pay him. I realized what a scum he was, how he had fooled me, made me . . . a plaything. But if I hadn't paid, he would have told your father." She rubbed her eyes and said querulously, "I had to pay him."

"Dad never knew?"

"Of course not," she said sharply. "Of course he didn't know."

"Was this what Francine Boutelle threatened to put in her story?"

Grace looked suddenly wary. It was interesting, watching her try to think. Slowly, she nodded.

"Did it ever occur to you," I asked, "that Boutelle may have already written the article?"

Sheer panic flooded Grace's face. "But she promised me . . ." Grace broke off sharply.

"What did she promise you?"

"I paid her and she promised not to put it in."

"Where did you get the money?"

"I put a mortgage on the lake-front house."

She had been able to pay off this time. With Dad dead, there was no one to question any financial transactions.

I frowned. The big meeting had been at Grace's house Monday night. I had my appointment to talk to Francine on Wednesday and it was Wednesday night that she was murdered.

"When did you pay her off?"

For the first time, Grace looked scared.

"Was it Wednesday? Did you go to her apartment Wednesday night?"

Grace folded her lips and looked stubborn.

"You'd better tell me, Grace. It's murder, you know."

"I have an alibi."

"Do you, indeed? That's interesting. Especially since they don't know when she was killed."

"She was still alive . . ." She clapped a hand over her mouth.

"When was she still alive, Grace?"

Grace looked at me uneasily. "I was there only a few minutes. She was fine when I left."

"What time was it?" I pressed.

"Just after six," Grace said reluctantly. "I stepped into her foyer and gave her the money. It was in a shoe box."

I could almost have smiled at that. How classic.

"Did she count it?"

"Yes. And then she promised me never to reveal . . . it."

Grace had asked me to go and see Francine, but she hadn't put any eggs in my basket. She would already have paid Francine before I had any opportunity to handle Francine. Another vote of confidence. But none of that mattered any more.

"You gave her fifty thousand in cash?"

Grace nodded.

"Grace, did you wear gloves when you put the money in the shoe box?"

Alarm flashed in her eyes. "No. Why?"

"I just wondered. If the police found it, I imagine they fingerprinted it."

Once again fear swept her. "What shall I do?"

"Do? Why, nothing, Grace. If I were you, I would do absolutely nothing." I stared at her for a long moment. "You've done enough damage, haven't you?"

I left then, left her to have her party, to wear her swirling blue silk dress. I drove down to the beach. I wanted to be alone and there is no place as lonely as a deserted beach at night. I parked and walked down winding wooden steps to a narrow strip of shore, still wet where the tide had eased out. I walked out to the end of the point and climbed a boulder and looked out in the darkness toward the ever-moving sea.

At least Dad never knew he had been betrayed. I think, perhaps, he might have felt pity at Grace's love affair, but he could never have forgiven the sale of his name. He had tried hard to be a good judge. I could hear Grace's self-pitying voice, "But really, K.C., what harm did it do? He had decided to suspend the sentence. The Levys could afford it. It didn't hurt anyone."

Oh, Grace.

And now, she had been at the doorstep of murder. I didn't fool myself. She was as close to it as anyone. I had started my search this afternoon, hoping to turn outward, away from the family, but it had come full circle. A closed circle.

Grace could have done it.

FIFTEEN

The phone was ringing when I got home.

"Hello."

"K.C." His voice was brusque and self-assured and I was surprised at the burst of pleasure it gave me to hear it.

"Yes, Harry."

"Did you see the news conference?"

So much had happened these last few hours that it took me a moment to remember.

"Oh no, I didn't." I had forgotten totally Kenneth's scheduled news conference. Had he expected me to come? "Did it go off all right?" I asked anxiously.

"Considering the circumstances, it went very well. Kenneth was subdued, but he sounded like an innocent man. He said he had found Francine Boutelle dead. He was so shocked that he didn't notify the police although he recognized now that he should have done so. He promised that he would testify fully at his trial and he felt confident he would be exonerated. He explained that he couldn't discuss the charge against him but he was innocent and, for that reason, he was refusing to relinquish his spot on the ticket although the state committee had asked him to step down." Harry paused. "I admired him."

I smiled. "Thank you, Harry."

"That's the good news."

"And the bad?"

"Farris is working overtime trying to figure out what Francine had on Kenneth. So far he hasn't come up with anything but he's sure he'll find it eventually. On the physical evidence, he has Carlisle cold. He has a witness placing him at the apartment and he has the scarf."

The scarf that Kenneth had removed from Francine's throat and put in his trunk.

Suddenly a thought occurred to me.

"Harry, what else did they find in Kenneth's trunk?"

"I don't think . . . wait a minute." Harry turned away from the receiver. "Hey, Paul. Paul, c'mere for a minute." There was a rustle, then, distantly, I heard Harry asking, "What did they find in Carlisle's trunk?" I couldn't hear the reply, then Harry said impatiently, "Yeah, yeah, I know. But what else?" A pause and he came back to the phone, "That's all, K.C. Just the scarf."

"But Harry, remember what that room looked like? It had been searched. And you told me they hadn't found a trace of the manuscript on the family. If it wasn't in Kenneth's car, that proves someone else was there."

I was excited, but I wanted to be sure. I called Kenneth.

He heard me out, then said quickly, "I didn't take a thing but the scarf." He sighed. "Of course, Farris has fastened on the scarf. As far as he is concerned that proves I did it. Then the money clinched it, for him."

"The money?"

"Yeah. I had fifty thousand in an envelope all ready for Francine. Fifty thousand dollar bills. I stuffed it in the car when I came back out. The police found that, too."

"They didn't find the manuscript?"

He was impatient. "No. I didn't take anything like that."

I asked him to go through his arrival again. "What time was it?"

"The clock struck seven as I was there. I remember it scared me when it started to sound."

Kenneth had been scared. It had been his breathing we had heard on the tape.

"Kenneth, this is important, really important. Was her desk messed up when you came? Had it been searched?"

"Yes," he said indifferently. To him, the clutter of the room was meaningless. All he could see was that white scarf. To me, it meant the murderer had already come.

I called Farris. He wasn't in. I asked for his home number.

"Captain, this is K.C. Carlisle, Kenneth Carlisle's lawyer."

"Office hours are nine to five, Miss Carlisle."

"Wait. This might be important. Captain, what did your men find in Kenneth's car?"

He thought it over for a long moment. It wasn't in his nature to trust a defense lawyer or to share any of the evidence. "It's up to the DA to release that information."

"I've heard they found the scarf and an envelope with fifty thousand dollars—and that's all."

He didn't answer.

"If that's true," I said urgently, "it proves someone else was there before Kenneth and that she was dead when he got there."

"Why?"

"Because the living-room had been searched. Obviously, some things are missing, probably the manuscript she was working on when she was killed. If Kenneth had taken anything, it would have been in the trunk with that scarf."

"Who says? Maybe he went by his office and threw it in the shredder. Maybe he dumped it in the corner trash. Maybe he ate it."

"For God's sake," I said angrily, "use your head. Why would he keep that damned scarf? Obviously, only because he had no chance to get rid of it. All right, if he didn't get rid of it, then he had no chance to get rid of a manuscript."

I didn't make any headway with Farris. None at all.

But I knew. After I hung up, I clung to that. I knew someone had been there before Kenneth. I knew one thing more. The killer must have taken Grace's fifty thousand dollars in the shoe box. I could be sure of that. It would have been blazoned in the news stories if a shoe box with fifty thousand dollars had been found in Francine's apartment.

Fifty thousand dollars and a manuscript had been there at six o'clock. Kenneth came at seven. Both were gone and Francine was dead.

It told me two things. The killer was greedy—and the manuscript must have posed a threat, which brought it neatly back to the Carlisles.

My head ached. I gently rubbed my temples then decided to shower and go to bed. I showered and slipped on a gown and fixed a scotch and soda. Then I flicked on the ten o'clock news. Kenneth's face, haggard and drawn, filled the screen. He was saying, ". . . and I pledge to the voters of this district that I am innocent. For that reason, I will continue my race and trust in the future." The film clip ended and the camera focused live on the news desk. A sweet-faced girl said briskly, "Carlisle's political foe, Greg Garrison, pledged tonight to keep the race on a high level." A film clip of Greg filled the screen. He was vividly handsome in the bright TV colors. He was shaking hands at a rally and turning to answer a question, "No, of course not. I don't intend to try and capitalize on Carlisle's problems. A man is innocent in this country until he is proven guilty. So we won't be mentioning the murder. The critical point is that I can better represent this district in Congress and that's what I intend to tell the voters."

The scene dissolved and the girl continued, "The cost-of-living index figures released today in Washington, D.C., indicate . . ."

I turned off the set. Greg, as always, radiated excitement and vigor. Perhaps he would sweep the campaign no matter what happened to Kenneth.

Frankly, I didn't give a damn about the campaign. What mattered now was to save Kenneth from prison. He didn't, under the particular requirements of California law, qualify for the gas chamber. But what difference did that really make? Conviction would be a death for him.

If it came to a trial . . . Dear God, I hoped not. A murder trial is the most grueling contest in the world. Day after day of strain and fear and pressure and, ultimately, a man will die or go to prison for the rest of his life—or be freed. It is hard on everyone involved, the judge, the jurors, the defendant, the prosecutor, the defense attorney.

I finished my drink, put on a tape of Debussy and settled on the couch with my legal pad. Kenneth would stand trial—unless I found the murderer first.

I renewed that pledge to myself the next morning as I stood at the side of an open grave and looked at Amanda's coffin. Amanda would expect it of me. She always trusted me to do my best. I would do it for her now, no matter what the cost.

The crowd was slimmer at the graveside than at the church. Rudolph and his family were there, of course, and some of Amanda's friends from her church circle and Kenneth and Megan and me. We were the only ones from the family.

After the last prayer, as the mourners began to straggle down the hill toward their cars, Kenneth and Megan came up to me. Kenneth slipped his arm around my shoulders, gave them a hard squeeze. We didn't speak. We didn't need to.

I drove back to my office. Once at my desk, I studied the plan of attack I had sketched on my legal pad last night. It seemed meager this morning, but it was all I had. I called John Solomon and asked him to have Pamela continue her search for the men in Boutelle's life. I called Priscilla, Edmond, and Travis and made appointments to see each. None was especially eager to talk to me.

Travis was still at Mother's. I met him in the library.

"Sad thing about old Kenneth, isn't it?" Travis observed, trying to look suitably serious and sorrowful.

"He's innocent."

Travis looked at me searchingly. "I'm sure that's the proper response, family and all, but, just between the two of us, they about caught him in the act, didn't they?"

"She was dead when Kenneth got there."

"Well, it's a pretty sticky wicket. Hope you can help the old fellow out."

"I intend to. For starters, where were you Wednesday night?"

Travis managed a not very friendly smile. "Not a very sisterly question."

"No."

"I'm pretty well out of it, old thing. I took Lorraine out to catch a plane back to Chicago. She had some surgery scheduled."

"What time did her plane leave?"

"Sixish."

Six. He would have had plenty of time.

"Why are you still here in La Luz, Travis?"

"Well, uh, I thought I should spend a little time with mater. I haven't seen so much of her these late years."

No, he hadn't. Travis, as perhaps even he recognized, scarcely ever had thoughts for anyone other than himself—or Lorraine.

I had given a little thought to Travis. He had two passions in life, antiquities and Lorraine. He had never really had the money to satisfy the first.

"Francine put it all in writing about you, Travis."

He no longer looked genial, pleasant or professorial. "What are you talking about?" he asked angrily.

"You didn't know?" I raised an inquiring eyebrow. "She had finished the section on you. All about the . . . I don't know just how it would be described in the art world, but . . ."

He reached out, grabbed my arm in a grip that hurt. "Will it get out, K.C.? Will it be in the papers?"

"I don't know, Travis. Of course, I will do my best to keep it quiet. Tell me everything that happened and I'll see what I can do." I shrugged free from his grasp.

"I thought I was safe. I thought no one would ever know."

It wasn't cold in the library, but I suddenly felt cold. Why had Travis been sure he was safe? Because Francine was dead?

He looked at me imploringly. "Don't look at me like that. That's like Lorraine. She's so damn rigid about things. K.C., you've got to help me. If Lorraine ever finds out, she'll leave me." He slammed a fist onto the table. "It's not like I'm really a crook. Hell, those greedy uneducated fools don't deserve to have fine art objects, anyway."

I understood. "You've provided some fakes, is that it? Sold forgeries to rich people who don't know any better?"

"Sure. It's easy. Easy as rolling off a log. Those damn people, the rich oil men from the Sun Belt, they don't know anything. They want a Ming vase. All right, I'll get them a Ming vase."

"You take your profits and have money to buy what you want."

"Beautiful things," he said softly, "lovely things."

"How did Francine find out?"

"I'll be damned if I know," Travis said slowly. "A couple of years back, I sold a Mayan figurine to Joe Seltzer here in town. He figured out it was a fake and took it to the DA but I managed to convince Seltzer I'd been fooled, too, and I repaid him. I didn't think anybody knew about it. It wasn't in the papers." He paused. "Lorraine was in London, attending a surgeons' seminar."

But Francine had discovered his secret. Worse, she had followed up some of his sales in recent years, obtained photographs of the works, and threatened to submit them to museum authorities.

"She could have ruined me," Travis said heavily. "And I would have lost Lorraine, too." He looked at me anxiously. "Where is the story? Who has it?"

"The police have one copy, I've heard. Of course, I don't know whether it contains that section on you." Now that I had it well baited, I sprung the trap. "But, look, Travis, when you paid her off Wednesday night, she probably destroyed the section on you."

"Oh hell no," he moaned. "She was already dead. I didn't . . ."

He stopped short.

"What time were you there, Travis?"

It was very quiet in the room. I realized suddenly just how big and powerful Travis was. He stood a head taller than I. He had strong shoulders and long arms and powerful hands.

"What are you up to?" His voice was hard.

"I'm trying to find out who killed Francine."

"I didn't kill her."

"I didn't say you did." You could have, I thought. "Look, Travis, the more I know, the more chance I will have to help Kenneth."

"Sure," he said. "I understand that. You want to get Kenneth out of a hole." He stared at me coldly. "Well, let me tell you something, little sister, you aren't going to put me in Kenneth's place," and he turned and slammed out of the library.

I drove next to Edmond and Sue's house. They invited me into their cheerful daisy-yellow breakfast room and offered me coffee. I accepted and there was an awkward silence.

They say old married couples look alike. There is something to it. Edmond has a narrow gentle face. Sue is his smaller, feminine image. They both stared at me worriedly, their faces pale and tense.

"You want to talk to us," Edmond said finally, putting his coffee cup down with a nervous rattle, "about that Boutelle woman?"

"Yes." I laid it on the table, "She was trying to blackmail you, too, Edmond."

"Yes."

I had to admire that quiet answer. He was a sensitive man, a retiring man, contending with a force beyond his experience.

"She was evil." Sue's face flushed, her voice shook. "I could have . . ."

"Sue." Edmond said sharply.

I stared at Sue. A pulse throbbed in her throat. The flush faded away, left her grey and trembling.

Edmond jumped up, moved to her side. "Sue, please, you will make yourself sick. Let me help you to your room." He glanced at me. "A moment, K.C., I'll be back in a moment."

His arm protectively around her, Edmond led her from the room. He was gone a few minutes, five or so, and, when he returned, his face was creased with worry. "Sue isn't strong, you know. She's had one heart attack and this is upsetting her."

"I'm sorry, Edmond. I didn't know or I would have spoken to you privately. I do need help. I must find out what Boutelle was up to, if I am to help Kenneth."

Edmond brushed a hand through his thinning hair. "I'm sorry I hadn't asked. How is Kenneth? Do you think it will work out all right?"

I suppose Edmond had spent his life with euphemisms. I was not in a mood to be euphemistic.

"Do you mean, do I think he will go to prison? Right now, I'd say it looks like it. The only hope he has is for me to find out who killed Francine."

Edmond stared down at the clear glass of the breakfast room table. "She was an evil woman."

"Did you go to her apartment Wednesday night to pay her off?"

"No. I was supposed to go. I had an appointment at six-thirty."

So another Carlisle had been scheduled to appear, cash in hand. Francine obviously had set up our visits on a staggered schedule and intended to lay back and watch the money roll in.

"Why didn't you go?"

"I felt that since we, the family, had asked you to meet with her that night, I should wait to see the results."

How nice of Edmond. So far as I had been able to determine, he was the only one who had followed the plan.

"Moreover," he said quietly, "I decided it was immoral to succumb to her threats. You see, I had not done anything wrong."

I waited.

"It is embarrassing to explain but I shall tell you and then you will understand that I really had nothing to fear. Just unpleasant publicity."

Unpleasant, indeed. For a man of Edmond's background and temperament, devastating publicity.

Edmond had, for years, enjoyed walking through La Pluma Park. The park had been, at one time, the pride of La Luz, but, of late years, it had become a rendezvous for drug users and homosexuals. Of this, Edmond was unaware. Three years earlier, he had been taking his customary walk, just at dusk. Suddenly he heard shouts and the sound of gunfire. Edmond stopped beneath a towering pine and wondered what to do. In a moment, a young man, dressed in corduroy shorts, tennis shoes and a t-shirt, ran lightly up the path. He was looking back and he ran into Edmond. As they picked themselves up, Edmond asked what was happening. The young man shrugged, "I dunno, mister. I heard shots and decided to get the hell out. Hey, here come some cops. Let's see what's going on."

As the police came closer, the young man abruptly began to run toward them. "Hey, man," he called out. "Help. This old fag's giving me the make. He dropped his pants."

Before Edmond could protest, he was under arrest for indecent exposure and lewd solicitation. He spent the night in the drunk tank, too stunned to call Sue or anyone.

"What happened?"

"I called Jim Holloway the next morning. He got me out of jail. Then, it turned out the charges were dropped because the complaining witness had given a false address and he never did show up for the trial. Jim thought probably the kid had been running to get away from a drug bust, they picked up eighty thousand worth of cocaine in the park that night, and he was diverting the police from himself."

It was just wild enough to be true, but that didn't wipe out the record of Edmond's arrest on charges that would destroy his social standing, humiliate his family, and wound his pride, should they be published.

"You decided just to let it all hang out, to let Francine publish and be damned?"

Edmond paused. "I had begun efforts to buy the magazine."

Surely Edmond and Sue weren't naive enough to believe that would be the end of it?

He hesitated, asked quietly, "Do the police know this?"

"I don't think so. Yet."

"Are you going to tell them?"

"Not unless I should determine it would be in Kenneth's interests for me to do so." That would only be if I decided Edmond was the killer. I didn't say that.

I left Edmond slumped in his light and airy breakfast room, looking out through glistening glass panes at an expanse of exquisitely groomed grass and tropical shrubs, wondering, perhaps, who had loosed the serpent in his Eden.

As I was driving to Priscilla's, I turned on the radio to catch the latest news. But Kenneth had been pushed out of first place, an excited announcer reporting that the body of an unidentified woman had been found in La Pluma Park. She was a well-nourished female in her middle twenties. She had been strangled.

"Police indicate death occurred sometime yesterday. The murder is the second this week in La Luz, an all-time record for homicides. In state news, flood waters are receding . . ."

I turned off the radio and wondered how best to approach Priscilla.

Priscilla wasn't in any mood to talk to me. She stood in her doorway, "I don't have time to talk today. Like I told you on the phone, I don't know a thing about Kenneth or what he's been doing lately."

She started to close the door.

I said briskly, "Wait a minute, Prissy. I know you were at Boutelle's apartment Wednesday night." It was a guess but I felt pretty confident Prissy would have been included in the roll call of Carlisles that evening.

The door stopped. She stared at me, her pale blue eyes hostile. She looked spectacular this morning, her color as rich as fresh cream, her hair a shining loose golden blonde, her mouth moist with red lip gloss.

"Fuck," she said quietly in her soft husky voice.

It was as obscene, that expletive coming from between those perfectly painted lips on that fresh young face, as graffiti on a Christmas card.

Abruptly, she shrugged. "All right. Come in." She led the way to the living room but she didn't ask me to sit down.

"Who saw me?"

"A neighbor."

She thought about it. "I can say he's a damned liar."

"Come off it, Prissy. You're pretty memorable."

That flattered her. "Okay," she said finally, "I was there. So what? She was dead. Damned dead."

"What time?"

"Why should I tell you?"

"I'm trying to help Kenneth."

She took her time. She wasn't, obviously, swept by sisterly concern.

"Look, K.C., I'll tell you—but if you repeat it, I'll deny every word of it. It was about six-forty-five."

"Did you knock or . . ."

"The door was open," she said carefully. "Wide open. Like I was supposed to come on in. I did. I stood in that little hall for a minute and it felt creepy, really creepy. I yelled out, 'Hey, where are you?' but it was quiet. Too damn quiet. I started to back out then, I don't know, I guess I was curious, I thought, hell, I'll just take a look around."

I could interpret that. Prissy might not be too brainy, but she was shrewd. She thought she was in an empty apartment with a golden chance to look around for that famous manuscript.

"I took a few steps into the living room. God. She looked awful."

"What did you do then?"

"I got out. I got the hell out."

I asked the next question very carefully.

"Okay, Prissy, pretend you're standing in that little hall. I want you to think about it, remember it."

She looked at me warily, but nodded.

"Okay, Prissy, what do you see from where you are standing?"

"A big chair," she said slowly. "It was blue. And a big fat rubber-tree plant and her desk."

"That's good, Prissy, really good." But not a word about drawers being pulled out, papers askew. "Okay, Prissy, what did you do with the manuscript and tapes?"

She backed away from me, reached out to grip the mantel over the fireplace. "Go to hell, K.C."

"You're going to tell me, Prissy."

She stood, her mouth a tight line, and shook her head.

"Yes, you are, because I've recorded every word you've said and, if you don't cooperate, I'm going to play it for the cops."

It wasn't nice. I didn't feel nice. I kept remembering the look on Kenneth's face before he turned to go up the walk to meet Megan.

Prissy turned and walked blindly toward the liquor cabinet. She sloshed whisky into a tumbler, raised it, and drank it half down before she turned to face me.

"K.C.," and her husky voice was hard, "you are a bitch."

"Let's not fight, Pris," I said tiredly. "I'll protect you, but I have to know exactly what happened. You got there and Boutelle was dead so you decided to look around and see if you could find the manuscript. Is that right?"

Sullenly, she nodded.

"That was good thinking, Pris," I said encouragingly. "Did you find it?"

My praise threw her off. "Yes," she said uncertainly. Then, eagerly, "It was sitting on her desk, the final copy and the carbon. I grabbed them up and then I looked on her desk and there were a bunch of cassettes with the name Carlisle on them. I rummaged through the drawers, looking to see if there were anything else, but I didn't find anything."

So it was Prissy who had searched the room, taken the manuscript and tapes. And Grace's fifty thousand?

"There was a shoe box," I said carefully. "It had some money in it. Did you take that?"

She frowned. "I didn't see a shoe box."

When Prissy came, Francine was dead and the shoe box gone. Could it have been murder for profit, after all? I felt a surge of hope. Then I remembered Kenneth's scarf. It couldn't have been murder for theft. The scarf had to be explained.

I considered the timing. Grace came at six, paid her money and left. According to her, Francine was alive. I didn't know when Travis had come. Edmond and Sue claimed they had not come. Prissy said she came at six-forty-five. According to her, the murderer took Grace's money but left the manuscript. Now, that was funny, wasn't it? After all, the manuscript threatened all of us . . .

"K.C., what are you going to do now?"

She stood between me and the door. One hand rested on the neck of a heavy cut-glass decanter. The sun streamed through a window behind her. I saw her through a glare. She looked indistinct and larger even than she was. And Priscilla was not small.

"I don't know, Pris, I'll have to think about all this. Now, why don't you give me all the stuff you took . . . ?"

She laughed, a throaty satisfied laugh. "I'm not so damn dumb. There isn't a scrap left. I burned the papers and mashed the ashes. I tore the tapes to pieces, then I burned them, too." She wrinkled her nose. "They smelled." She laughed again. "I played them first. I'll have to say that bitch knew how to find things out. Did you know they caught old cousin Edmond with his pants down in the park? And it turns out Cousin Travis is a fraud and you," and she glared at me, hostility naked in her eyes, "and you, clever clever K.C., you tipped Sheila out of the boat, didn't you?"

Shock roared in my ears. So that had been Francine's game. Not the truth, that Sheila had pulled away, leaving me to drown. No, she had twisted it, turned it, would have left me dangling in the wind as my sister's killer,

"And Grace," Priscilla continued shrilly, "oh, how I would have loved to see that printed. Righteous Grace and her roll in the hay."

"But Priscilla," I interrupted sharply, "you've forgotten something!"

"Forgotten?"

"Yes, you've forgotten yourself. She really had the goods on you."

Priscilla raised the decanter. It glittered richly in the sunlight. She pulled the stopper and once again filled her glass. She took a deep swallow.

"Maybe she did," Priscilla said thickly, "but it didn't do her any damned good. I've got the picture now and I burned it and the negative and nobody will ever know."

Picture, picture, picture. Something teased at my brain, wavered in my memory. Picture. But what the hell was it?

"Yeah," she said heavily, "and that's the only picture there ever was, that one in the *Beacon.*"

I remembered. Amanda had sent me the clipping. "Poor Miss Prissy," Amanda had written, "I'm so afraid she will never learn to know good people from bad. She has had such a narrow escape but it's an awful thing . . ."

I looked at Prissy, standing there swaying, holding the decanter, now tipping it again to refill her glass. Beautiful Priscilla with her clear lovely skin and china blue eyes. Everyone always made excuses for her, blamed her mistakes on her "crowd." The picture had been a dreadful one, the sleek rounded body of the sports car tilted crazily against a brick wall, and, starkly pitiful against the pavement, three sheeted figures. Such small sheeted figures. Children's bodies.

I didn't remember the details of the picture now, though I dimly recalled the driver's door had hung open. I did recall the headline:

CHILDREN RUN DOWN, DRUNK DRIVER DIES; PASSENGER THROWN

Prissy had been the passenger. It was her car but Jimmy Fremont was driving. An all-night party and Jimmy had driven through a school zone and two little brothers and their friend died. Prissy left town, went to Acapulco for a year to avoid questions about why she had let a drunk drive.

"So that was it," I said quietly. "Jimmy wasn't driving, after all, was he, Prissy? And you were drunk, too."

She stared at me a long moment, her face heavy with drink, then slowly, sickeningly, she began to laugh. "I fooled them all, didn't I?"

"You didn't fool Francine."

The laughter stopped. Black anger twisted Prissy's face. "That bitch. She brought me the picture, showed it to me."

Francine made Prissy understand that the picture proved it was impossible for Jimmy to have been driving. There had been time, after the crash, for Priscilla, with minor injuries, to climb out of the upended car and stagger to the sidewalk. But Jimmy's body was beneath the car and it could have been wedged there only if he tumbled from the passenger seat as the car began to tip.

How had the police missed it then?

Prissy shrugged. "Those little kids . . . The mother of one of them came and she screamed and screamed . . . and Jimmy was still alive, see, right after it happened, so they lifted the car and pulled him out from under, then nobody thought about it because I said he was the driver, of course."

Of course. That was Prissy. She could kill little kids and in the next breath be busy saving herself.

Perhaps Francine had run into a tougher customer than she had expected.

SIXTEEN

I drove to my office, told Pat to bar the door and sat down to think.

First, I listed the suspects.

Grace.

Priscilla.

Edmond and Sue.

Travis.

Kenneth.

Myself.

Then—and did I do it reluctantly?—I put down Harry's name. He had been at the scene of the crime. If he were the murderer, he could have waited nearby and followed me onto the scene to be sure that the murder was reported then.

What would be the point of that?

For one thing, it was he who had the letter, purportedly from Francine, that directed the police to Kenneth.

But I had no reason to believe Harry knew Francine or could have any motive for murdering her.

Could he be Francine's Mr. Wonderful? Could he be Francine's link to La Luz? He would certainly have the kinds of information that could have led Francine to the sorry secrets of the Carlisles.

If only I knew more about Francine.

Impatiently, I called John Solomon's office.

"No, Pamela's not in. She's still working on the Boutelle case for you."

"Has she come up with anything else on Boutelle's boyfriend?"

"Not yet. She's trying to get in touch with Boutelle's best friend at the Cocoa Butter, but so far she hasn't found the woman at home. Course, with that kind of gal, who knows when she might come home. You still interested?"

"Yes. Have her keep after it. I'll check back later today. When you talk to her, get the woman's name and address."

It sounded like the best bet for information. It was from the Cocoa Butter that Francine had come to La Luz. Francine. Bright, beautiful, unprincipled. What had lured her from the Cocoa Butter to La Luz—and death?

On the surface, it was to write a story about the Carlisles. But why had she wanted to do that? Was it just to make a fast buck? Maybe. But why the Carlisles? Until Kenneth went into politics, the Carlisles weren't at all well known beyond the confines of this little coastal town. How could Francine have come up with the dirt on each of us? It suggested a long and intimate acquaintance with La Luz or the family but so far as John Solomon and Pamela had been able to discover, Francine had never in her life been to La Luz until she showed up six weeks ago.

Six weeks to death.

It would never have occurred to Francine, young and sensuous, vibrantly, crudely alive, in love with a 'magical' man, that she had an early appointment with death. It must have been quite a surprise when death reached out to her.

Francine came to La Luz and died because she threatened to write a story detailing the sins and follies of my family.

I sighed. No matter how I looked at it, it always came back to the Carlisles.

All right, turn it around. Who profited from Francine's death?

Grace. Priscilla. Travis. Edmond and Sue. Kenneth. Myself.

But only because Priscilla lifted the manuscript and the tapes.

What then did the murder itself accomplish?

Most obviously, it removed Francine. It resulted in Kenneth's arrest.

Wearily, I poured a cup of coffee from my desk thermos and stirred it slowly. The coffee was murky, murky as my thoughts.

The scarf. That was critical, of course. If Kenneth were innocent, it meant the scarf was deliberately taken with murder in view and the ultimate goal of saddling Kenneth with the crime. I tried to picture Travis, hearty red-bearded Travis, opening the cloakroom at Kenneth's office, looking swiftly around, then reaching out to grab Kenneth's scarf. Or Priscilla? Or Edmond?

The scarf, if Kenneth were innocent, meant that death had stalked Francine all that day. It was no spur-of-the-moment, angry attack. It was cool and deliberate and planned.

Their faces, the faces of my kin, moved in my mind. Imperious Grace, greedy Travis, retiring Edmond, selfish Priscilla, confident Kenneth.

Suddenly, I felt very discouraged. I wasn't getting anywhere. I could posit from here to Christmas, and one theory would be as good or as bad as another. I had no proof and I had no inkling who was the murderer.

I picked up my pen and made a series of heavy dark XXXXXs across the face of my pad. Nothing, it all came to nothing. But pettish scrawls on a legal pad weren't going to help Kenneth. Grimly, I tried again. What did I know?

Francine Boutelle was alive at six.

Grace came at six, paid, left.

Then came Travis or Priscilla, I was uncertain in what order.

I picked up the phone and dialed Grace's. Travis was wary.

"I don't admit to anything."

"Travis, stuff it. Just answer two questions, yes or no. When you came to a certain apartment Wednesday night, did you see a shoe box sitting on the desk?"

"A shoe box?" I could tell from his tone he thought I was crazy and that convinced me he had not seen Grace's shoe box or the fifty thousand it held.

"No, sis, I didn't see a shoe box." He was relaxed now, amused. I wasn't a threat.

"Okay. One final question. Was the room in disarray? Did it look like it had been searched?"

He was cautious with this one, uncertain of its meaning. "Yes," he said finally.

"Thanks, Travis."

I hung up and wrote quickly on my pad, for his answers clarified the order of appearance.

Grace at six.

Priscilla at six-forty-five.

Kenneth at seven.

Travis next.

Me. Then Harry.

If I accepted everything I had been told, the shoe box was gone when Priscilla came. But the manuscript and tapes were there.

The last puzzled me. Why? Had the murderer been frightened away before grabbing up the manuscript and tapes? Maybe. But it would be pretty dumb to kill someone to hide certain facts then leave, for the police to find, a manuscript containing the blackmail material. Panic? Somehow, I didn't think the hands that had so skillfully and mercilessly dropped a scarf around Francine's neck and pulled it inexorably tight would be prone to panic.

I pushed up from my desk, began to pace.

Try another tack. Think of the night from Francine's point of view. She had gone to a lot of effort, organizing that night. She had arranged for her victims to come, one after another, bringing pay-off money. If she had lived the night, she would have been rich. Grace brought and left fifty thousand. Priscilla, Kenneth, and Travis all came with fifty thousand, but didn't, of course, leave the money because Francine was dead.

But Francine didn't live the night. She died sometime between six and seven. That we knew as a fact because the tape recorder came on at seven o'clock. It recorded Kenneth's frantic effort to loosen the scarf, Travis's arrival and cautious survey, and my coming and Harry's.

If only the murder had happened after seven, then it would have been captured on tape. It was bad luck that the murderer had chosen an earlier time . . .

I stopped walking, pressed my fingers against my temples. Grace's money . . . seven o'clock . . . no record from six to seven . . . no record from six to seven . . .

My chest ached. I tried to breathe, tried to think beyond the enormity of that statement, no record from six to seven.

It all fell into place, all the odd-shaped pieces that hadn't quite fitted the puzzle. It was quite simple and perfect and sickening.

I sank into my chair. My mind pulsed with thoughts and conjectures and guesses, but they all came together. Now everything made sense. I knew how Francine Boutelle knew so many facts about the Carlisles. I knew why Kenneth was the goat.

Francine had made a very basic mistake. She had trusted the wrong person. Death must indeed have been a surprise.

The objective of the killer had been two-fold, to be freed from Francine and to injure the Carlisles. The murderer had succeeded absolutely—and there wasn't a vestige of proof that I could offer. It would be my word against the killer's.

But there must be a way, now that I knew . . .

The phone rang. It was Kenneth and he was upset. "I want you to talk some sense into Megan."

"What's wrong?" I was impatient. I didn't have time for this.

"I want her to go to Laguna, stay with her folks. I'm afraid for her."

"Why?"

"A man called here last night. He spoke in a thick German accent. He asked Megan to report to the hospital, there had been an emergency, a bus load of people hurt on the edge of town and they were calling in volunteers to help. Megan went, but it was a hoax."

"A hoax?"

"Yes. She got to the hospital and nothing had happened and no one there had called her. When she came back out to the car, she had a flat tire. And, damn it, she didn't call me. I had gone on to bed. She didn't get home for a couple of hours."

"She wasn't hurt? Nobody threatened her or anything?"

"No, but I don't like it. It's damned odd."

It was odd but not, in the scheme of things, too important. "I wouldn't worry, Kenneth. Megan's okay and after this, she can be more careful about responding to phone requests. But she ought to stay here. It will look odd if she leaves La Luz now. Besides, she really should show up with you tonight at the debate."

"That's what she says," he agreed reluctantly. "But I don't like it."

I soothed him finally. I asked him to call his office staff and tell them I would be coming by and that I had his permission to talk to them.

"Sure. But why?"

"The scarf, Kenneth."

"Oh yeah." His voice was flat, the reminder not a cheerful one. "K.C., have you discovered anything?"

"I'm getting close, Kenneth. I have to find out a little more."

"Sure," he said again. I knew he didn't, really, have much hope.

I didn't want to tell him yet. I was sure, but the scarf was a real stumbling-block. Everything fitted, in my new picture, except the scarf.

Kenneth's office staff was subdued, as might be expected. I asked all of them, the office manager, twelve secretaries, four paralegals and the kitchen help, to come into the main conference room.

"I appreciate all of your taking time to talk to me. I don't know if you all know of the difficulty Mr. Carlisle is in?"

They knew. Some of them shifted uncomfortably, looked away, embarrassed.

"First, I want to make one point very clear. Mr. Carlisle is innocent." I said it firmly and looked at each of them in turn. "That's the most important thing to remember. Now, I know all of you would like to help him?"

Some nodded. Some murmured yes.

"Then listen very closely to what I have to say. It may make all the difference to him. First, do you know how Miss Boutelle was killed?"

One of the older secretaries nodded. "Strangled, Miss, that's what it said in the paper."

"That's right," I said approvingly. "She was strangled. But does anyone know what was used by the murderer?"

They looked at me, blank-faced. The scarf had not been mentioned in the news reports.

"Miss Boutelle was strangled with Mr. Carlisle's white silk scarf."

It was utterly quiet.

I tried to watch all of them at once. That isn't easy but when you've spent five years watching the faces in a jury, you widen your field of vision. I saw what I hoped to see.

"Now," I said slowly, "that sounds bad for Mr. Carlisle. And it is. The murderer planned it that way."

They were hanging on every word now and there was one face I watched especially closely.

"The murderer deliberately used Mr. Carlisle's scarf."

"But Miss Carlisle, how did he do that?" a paralegal asked.

"That's what I'm hoping one of you can tell me."

You could have heard a mouse sneeze.

"The scarf was here Monday morning. Last Monday. Do all of you remember Monday? That was the day several of the Carlisle family members were here for a meeting. The scarf was in Mr. Carlisle's coat pocket when he put it in the closet last Monday." I paused, said slowly, "It was not in his pocket when he left the office Monday afternoon."

There was an excited buzz.

"I'm hoping that one or several of you may be able to help me. I'm going to stay in the conference room after our meeting is over and I will be waiting to talk to anyone who knows anything about the scarf." I looked directly at a plump, pleasant-faced girl in her mid-twenties.

She lagged behind as everyone began to leave. I rose and closed the door and we faced each other.

"How did you know?" Tears welled in her eyes. "I never thought . . . I didn't mean . . ."

"I know you didn't," I said gently, "and your stepping forward now proves you didn't mean to cause any trouble for Mr. Carlisle."

"Oh, I didn't. Miss. It was . . . I thought it was some kind of a lark. She explained it to me that way."

"She?" For a moment, I wondered if I could have it wrong, all wrong.

"Yes, and you could have knocked me over with a feather when I saw her picture in the paper."

It was all incoherent and a little jumbled, but, in essence, the girl's story was simple enough.

Francine Boutelle had struck up a conversation with her over lunch one day in the drug store. Boutelle had expressed a lot of interest when she found out that Trudy worked in Kenneth Carlisle's office. Somehow, Trudy wasn't quite sure how, the conversation came around to the excitement of knowing celebrities, and Francine, though that was not the name she gave Trudy, confided that she collected things that belonged to famous people and, since it looked as if Kenneth might be going to Washington, she would like to have something of his for her collection. Something he wore. That stumped Trudy but Francine, after some thought, said what about that silk scarf he wore? If Trudy would get it for her, she would be willing to pay a nice sum. Fifty dollars or so.

Trudy was in tears by the time she finished. I assured her she wouldn't lose her job and asked her not to tell anyone of our talk but to be ready to give her testimony to the authorities. Not, of course, that I thought such testimony from an employee of Kenneth's would be enough to persuade Farris, but ultimately I was going to have enough evidence.

After Trudy left, I sat for a few minutes longer in the conference room. The killer was clever, cleverer even than I had imagined, still a vague and faceless creature hiding behind Francine.

How had Francine been persuaded to obtain the instrument of her destruction? Did she think the scarf would be used as some kind of evidence that Carlisle had come to her apartment, made a pay-off? Because, of course, she thought she and Mr. Wonderful would share all the money reaped from Carlisles and, at the same time, enjoy humbling the hated family.

For a moment, I felt a surge of sympathy for Francine. Then I remembered Amanda. Francine, because she had so few scruples, so little compassion, had destroyed Amanda. She had been willing to destroy anyone for her own gain. What she cannot have realized, until that last dreadful moment, was that she too was slated for destruction.

The killer, from the moment of meeting her and learning of her background, must have planned to use her to injure the Carlisles. He had not counted on Francine falling in love with him—and he was determined, at all costs, at any cost, to avoid marriage.

I was the only person in the world who knew who he was. But somewhere he must have left a trail that I could find.

I called Pamela.

She was a little defensive. "Gee, I'm sorry, K.C. I wish I had been able to come up with more. I know you need all the help you can get."

"You've done a good job, Pamela. I want the name and address of Francine's friend at the Cocoa Butter."

"Sure. Hold on a minute." She came back with a name and address. "I've been down there twice, K.C. Nobody answers the door. The neighbors don't know and the manager of the Cocoa Butter is furious. She didn't show up Thursday night."

I wrote down the name, Kristy Gale, and the address in Huntington Beach. It was a fanciful name, of course, like so many girls who work in clubs. Her real name was probably Christine. I was pinning a lot of hope on Miss Gale. If she were really a close friend of Francine's, there was the chance she had seen Mr. Wonderful. All I needed was a description.

Maybe she would be home now. I frowned. So she hadn't shown up for work Thursday night. The news of Francine's murder hit the late morning and early afternoon editions of papers all up and down the coast. Had Kristy Gale seen the news?

Then, more disturbingly, I wondered what she might have done. If she knew Francine's lover, she might have called him; asked, perhaps, if he wanted to help with the funeral arrangements.

It would have shocked him, wouldn't it, when he thought his traces were so well covered.

SEVENTEEN

Traffic is always heavy on the coastal highway but I made it down to Huntington Beach in two hours. I drove too fast, driven by fear of what I might find. Then I would reassure myself. I had lived with high drama so many hours that I was losing my perspective.

I found the house, just a few blocks off the main street. The modest stucco houses with palmetto palms and tiny grass plots looked a little down-at-heel. Kristy's house was in mid-block.

It was late afternoon. Four boys played touch football in the middle of the street. Television screens flickered in living rooms. An old man gardened next door. He stopped to watch me walk up on the front porch.

I knocked.

The old man leaned on his hoe, fixed me with an unwavering gaze.

I knocked again and wished a hole would swallow him up. How was I going to get in this house with him watching? I was determined to get inside. I was so absorbed I almost missed the tiny jerk of the living room drape.

The drape was still now, but I was sure it had moved. I felt a surge of excitement. Maybe Kristy Gale was here. Maybe she was safe, after all.

I knocked again, a determined knock.

The door began to open. It opened just enough for a frightened face to peer at me.

The shock of seeing her almost made me faint. I had thought the house was empty. And now, to see that unmistakable face.

I knew who she was, of course. There could be no mistake. I scrabbled in my mind for her name. What was it Kenneth had said?

"Kendra?" I whispered.

She pulled the door wider and looked at me hopefully. She looked so much like her father, the same sandy hair in small tight curls, the same broad generous face with a sprinkling of freckles, the same sea-green eyes.

"Did my mother send you?" Tears welled in her eyes. "Where's Mother? Where is my mother?"

"Oh Kendra, baby," I said gently, and I wrapped my arms around her and held her thin little body next to mine.

She knew then that Kristy (surely a dressier version of a girl who had grown up in La Luz as Christy Nelson) hadn't sent me.

Kendra pulled back, lifted a frightened tear-stained face. "Do you know where Mother is? She left Thursday afternoon. She said she was going to La Luz and then she would go to work. But Buddy called and he was real mad and he said Mother hadn't come to work. She hasn't called or come home or anything."

"No, Kendra," I said slowly, "I don't know where she is." But I was afraid, terribly afraid.

Then I asked gently, "Kendra, was she going to meet someone in La Luz?"

She nodded. "Yes. The man Franny went with."

I was close, so close.

"Do you know his name?"

Kendra frowned. "No. I don't think so."

My shoulders slumped.

"I saw him once. He and Franny came here late one night after Mother and Franny finished at the club. I was supposed to be asleep but they made a lot of noise, you know. Mother and her friends did, late at night," she said matter-of-factly, "and I wasn't supposed to come in. I think," she said painfully, "that Mother didn't want people to know she had a big kid like me. But sometimes, when I woke up, I would go outside and slip around and look in through the window, over there. Then I could see everybody and it was a lot of fun."

"Tell me, Kendra, what did he look like?"

She described him.

I didn't feel a rush of triumph. I felt, instead, sad and weary. For now I knew, beyond doubt. I had my link between Francine and La Luz. A double link, actually. Francine had known Kristy Gale. Had Kristy confided the truth of Kendra's parentage? Yes, she must have. Then, when Francine met Mr. Wonderful, she told him, "Oh, you'll be interested in this, you'll like knowing this." He had liked it a lot. Was that how the scheme was hatched? He would provide the dirt on the Carlisles and she would write the story, set them up for blackmail.

He hadn't counted on Francine falling in love with him. More than that, she wanted marriage.

Kendra was tugging at my hand. "Please, what am I going to do? Mother has never gone off and left me before. I don't know what to do until she comes back."

Until she comes back.

I took a deep breath. "Kendra, I don't know exactly what to say." God knows that was the truth. "Did your Mother ever tell you anything about your father?"

"Not a lot," Kendra said diffidently. "She said . . . well, Mother laughs and kids about things a lot. She's really a happy person. All she ever told me was that it wasn't exactly a mistake, but she and he didn't stick together and he didn't even know about me. She said when I was real old someday she would tell me. But," and Kendra said this quickly, "she said he was a real nice guy."

"Your mother must be real nice, too," I said gently.

Kendra smiled and for a moment her face didn't look pinched and frightened. "She is."

"Well, I'm glad she told you that because I'm your daddy's cousin. My name is K.C. I think I'd better take you home with me until we find out where your mother is."

Kendra was reluctant to leave, but I felt, every minute, a growing sense of danger. I had to find Kendra a safe place. It wasn't here. And I had a horrid fear that her mother was never coming home.

We were almost at the outskirts of La Luz when the music on the radio was interrupted by a bulletin.

"The body found yesterday in La Pluma Park has been identified as that of a former La Luz resident, Christy Nelson. La Luz police have announced that Kenneth Carlisle, released on bail yesterday on another murder charge, has been picked up for questioning in regard to the death of Miss Nelson." The announcer's voice quivered with excitement. This was as much scandal as had erupted in La Luz since the First Methodist choir director ran away with a high school senior. "Station KOKX will keep listeners informed when further news is released." The music picked up in mid-bar.

I slowed and turned into a parking lot.

Kendra huddled in the seat beside me. I reached out and put my arm around her. "I'm sorry, Kendra. I was afraid of this."

"Kenneth Carlisle?" She said it raggedly, as if each syllable hurt her throat.

"That's your daddy, honey, and he didn't hurt your mother. I promise you that. No, the man who killed your mother is the man she went to meet in La Luz yesterday, Franny's boyfriend."

"Can't we tell the police . . . ?"

"I don't know, Kendra. We don't have any proof."

"But I saw him, I know . . ."

"How can you be positive that's who your mother went to meet?"

Kendra screwed her face in thought. "Mother told me that she called the man, Franny's friend, to see if she could help him and he wanted her to come to La Luz."

Farris could say that Kendra would lie to protect her father, even a father she had never known. He would look at me and accuse me of orchestrating a defense.

"We have to do something," Kendra cried.

"We will," I said soberly. "Let me think."

Kendra was one tiny link to the killer, but a tenuous one. There was one more link, one mistake the killer had made, that couldn't be excused away. If I could just decide how to attack.

I drove across the parking lot to an outdoor phone and called Megan.

"K.C., thank God you've called! Have you heard . . . ?"

"Yes. But don't worry . . ."

"Don't worry?" Her voice shrilled with hysteria. "Don't worry? They say he killed that girl, the one in the park. An anonymous caller called the police and told them Kenneth was involved with her years ago and now they think he killed her and Francine to hide the fact that Christy had his baby. It happened last night when I was gone, at the hospital. I told them about that phone call, but they don't believe me . . .

"Megan, wait, listen to me."

She stopped and I could hear her ragged breathing.

"Megan, I need help. You've got to trust me. I know who the killer is but I've got to have your help. I have Kenneth's daughter here with me and I have to find her a safe place. If the murderer knew that she had seen him . . ."

"Of course, I'll help." The answer was swift and controlled, the Megan who could be counted on. "Bring her here."

Kendra and I slipped in the back way. Megan met us at the door. She took one look and stepped forward to take Kendra in her arms. "You poor darling. I'm sorry, I'm terribly sorry."

I left them getting acquainted in the kitchen and I went to the library and sat down at Kenneth's desk.

Megan came in a little later. "Kendra's in her bath. Isn't she a dear?"

"Yes. Yes, she is."

Megan paused then said uncertainly, "I don't want to bother you, K.C., and I suppose it doesn't matter now . . ."

"What doesn't matter?"

"The campaign."

Oh yes, Kenneth's campaign. But now he was in a race for his life. No, the campaign didn't matter much. If I could prove him innocent, I would at the same time save his political future. I wondered, when it was all over, if that would matter much to Kenneth?

"I don't know what to do. No one's shown up, none of his political friends," she said bitterly, "since he was arrested this afternoon. But the debate is supposed to start at nine. The TV station keeps calling and asking if someone is going to come in Kenneth's place."

The debate. Of course, the fall campaign had pointed toward tonight. Greg would be there. And Harry Nichols. The *Beacon* was sponsoring the debate and Harry would be the moderator.

The debate. Live before TV cameras on the stage of La Luz high school. Slowly, I began to smile.

Megan looked at me oddly.

"Don't cancel," I said abruptly, "I'll go. I'll take Kenneth's place."

" K.C., that's wonderful of you." Then her face fell. "But it doesn't really matter, does it?"

It might, I thought. It just might matter a lot.

Megan left me in the library, to make some plans for the debate. I ran through it in my mind. My plan was a gamble, but it might work. It had to work.

It was just after eight o'clock. It took me fifteen minutes to track down Capt. Farris.

When he knew it was me on the line, he said impatiently, "Look, Counselor, there's no point in your talking to me."

"Farris, you've got the wrong man."

"Tell it to the jury."

"No, I'm going to tell it to the entire city of La Luz. Tonight. At nine o'clock. And, Farris, the murderer may not like what I say so I would appreciate it if you would come. La Luz high school. Nine p.m."

"Oh, bullshit, Miss Carlisle . . ."

"If he kills me, it will be awkward for you, Captain." I hung up.

I just had time to go by my office, put it all on tape, then drive to the high school.

Harry Nichols was arriving at the same time. He wore a charcoal gray suit and a pale yellow shirt and a blue grey tie. His dark face turned toward me in surprise. The crowd surged between us and I hurried a little. I didn't want to talk to him now.

The lobby smelled of chalk dust and mold. I brushed past people beginning to straggle to their seats and went down the right aisle.

Greg was walking down the left aisle, stopping to greet friends and supporters along the way. He was taller than average. Handsome, vital Greg. Women clung to his hand, called after him.

I gained the stage and Harry was right behind me.

"Are you going to appear for Kenneth?" he asked.

I nodded. That was true. That was not all of it, but nothing more, obviously, had occurred to Harry.

Greg was in high good-humor by the time he gained the stage. It was only then that he saw me, standing by Kenneth's lectern.

For a moment, his face was blank, then he moved quickly toward me, and, ignoring the crowd, gave me a quick hug.

"Hey," he said good-humoredly, "I didn't bargain to take on the pretty Carlisle."

"Kenneth can't come," I said quietly.

Greg's face furrowed. "Yeah. I know. I heard on the radio. I'm damned sorry, K.C. But look, we'll just keep it on the issues tonight."

"Right."

Then the TV technicians were waving us to our places, holding up their light meters, flashing on the huge overhead lights.

Then the red lights glowed.

Harry began.

"Tonight the *Beacon* is hosting a debate between two candidates for Congress. On my left is Greg Garrison, attorney, former La Luz District Attorney, and present candidate. On my right we have a substitute for the candidate, Kenneth Carlisle, who has been unable to attend. In his place is his cousin, Miss K.C. Carlisle, a local attorney."

The audience applauded and craned to look at me and I knew the buzz of talk was not about politics.

"Each candidate," Harry continued, "will have three minutes to make a presentation and we will then submit in turn questions which have been drawn up by a panel of political experts. Speaking first will be Mr. Greg Garrison."

Greg was superb, projecting just enough sense of combat to be attractive. Never stuffy or banal, he came across as vigorous, articulate, persuasive.

When he finished, Harry turned to me.

I looked out at the sea of faces, then I began.

"My cousin, Kenneth Carlisle, is not here tonight because he is in jail."

There was a gasp, it sounded like the sea sucking at rocks as the tide races out.

"He is being held on a charge of murder. The second murder charge he has faced in a week."

Several thousand people watched me. I could feel their eyes.

"I want to tell you how this came about—and who planned and committed these murders."

I saw Harry's face jerk toward me.

"Six weeks ago, a woman came to town. Her name was Francine Boutelle. She was a night club dancer but, before that, she was a writer. A writer of exposes. But it was as a dancer that she made a friendship that would lead her to La Luz. She met a woman named Christy Nelson," the audience rustled, moved, "who had known Kenneth Carlisle years earlier. Kenneth was the father of Christy's ten-year-old daughter, although Kenneth wasn't to learn of the birth until Francine Boutelle told him. Francine knew of Kenneth's daughter from Christy. Francine thought this was interesting. She told it to a man she had met, an exciting and handsome man who lived in La Luz. They talked about this and about Francine's work as a writer and one day this man suggested that Francine write a story about the Carlisle family and sell it to *Inside Out, a* magazine that specializes in racy exposes. Francine quit her job at the night club and came to La Luz."

I said quietly, "Francine was very beautiful. She was young. She fell in love with the man from La Luz. She saw ahead a fantastic life, teamed with Mr. Wonderful. But he had other plans. So he devised a marvelous scheme. It would destroy a man he hated, Kenneth Carlisle, injure the Carlisle family, and free himself of Francine's unwanted devotion. It worked beautifully."

"I'm sorry," Greg interrupted, his voice good-humored but tinged with impatience, "I came here tonight to discuss political positions.

Although I can sympathize with Carlisle and his family on his current difficulty, I don't think this is the proper forum to hear about it."

"These people," and I waved my hand toward the audience, "want to know what happened. I'm going to tell them now how Francine died. Francine had arranged for various members of the Carlisle family to come to her apartment. She had demanded fifty thousand dollars from each of them and in return she promised not to publish various unpleasant things she knew about them.

"All of the Carlisles except Edmond and myself made preparations to pay Miss Boutelle. Meanwhile, Mr. Wonderful had arranged for Miss Boutelle herself to obtain from Mr. Kenneth Carlisle's office the scarf which was used to strangle her.

"At six o'clock Wednesday night, Grace Carlisle brought a shoe box with cash. She paid Miss Boutelle and left. Between then and six-forty-five when Miss Priscilla Carlisle arrived, Francine Boutelle was killed. Priscilla took the Carlisle manuscript and tapes. Then Kenneth arrived. Imagine his shock when he finds Miss Boutelle dead with his scarf around her neck. How would you feel if that happened to you?" I paused and it was utterly quiet.

Greg lounged back behind his lectern, a look of boredom on his face. Harry Nichols watched me intently.

"Kenneth made a mistake. He loosened the scarf, took it with him, and, when it was found in the trunk of his car, it resulted in his arrest."

I walked from behind the lectern, closer to the edge of the stage.

"Do you see now how it all happened? It was most marvelously set up. It was, from the killer's viewpoint, a fantastic success. Then yesterday afternoon his telephone rang. Christy Nelson called, saying she knew how close he was to Francine."

I grimaced for this was the coldest, most vicious act of all.

"That kindness of Miss Nelson's caused her death. She drove to La Luz Thursday afternoon and met our killer, who had carefully arranged to decoy Megan Carlisle out of her house so that Kenneth would have no alibi. The killer strangled Miss Nelson and dumped her body in La Pluma Park. Then he was sure he was safe."

Slowly I turned, walked back to the center of the stage, then again faced the audience.

"But he isn't safe. He stands here tonight, a man who hated the Carlisles, who wanted to make the Carlisles suffer."

Greg and Harry looked at me sharply.

"The murderer made one big mistake. Greed prompted it. As I mentioned earlier, Grace Carlisle brought fifty thousand dollars in a shoe box. The killer took that shoe box."

I walked toward him and looked into his face.

"It was clever, Greg, damned clever. But the police have a search warrant now and they are looking into your safety deposit box, your car, your campaign headquarters and when they find the money, you are finished. You didn't keep the box, of course, but Grace's fingerprints are on the bills."

EIGHTEEN

"How did you know?" Farris demanded.

"She died before seven o'clock."

"So?"

"Don't you see, the whole evening was arranged, and arranged long before that night, the scarf obtained, the Carlisles lined up like ducks and, finally, Harry Nichols set up to find the body and sic the police on Kenneth. If it had all gone on schedule, Greg would have had two hundred thousand in cash. If the original scenario had worked, Francine would have raked in the money from all of us then been killed just before Harry Nichols arrived."

"Instead she died before seven. Why?" Farris asked.

I looked at him ruefully. "I hope I don't go to jail."

"I'll be goddamned. The tape recorder."

I nodded. "Yeah. I planted it. Only three people in the world knew it was going to start recording at seven o'clock, John Solomon, me, and Greg."

It took a long time to sift it all out, tell Farris where to look for evidence. Then they found Grace's fifty thousand, stuffed in ski-boots in his closet.

It was long after midnight when Harry and I left the police station.

We drove without talking until we reached my apartment house. Then Harry said abruptly, "So you and Greg were . . . pretty close."

"Yes."

"I'm sorry."

"It's all right."

"Is it really?"

I thought of Amanda and Kendra's mother. "Yes, Harry," I said steadily, "it really is."

He parked the car, started to get out.

"You don't need to walk me to the door."

"Of course I do."

I didn't say anything, just smiled a little in the darkness. Harry would always do it his way.

I wondered what he would think if I told him I had thought, at one time, that he might be Francine's Mr. Wonderful?

I didn't plan to tell him that. It's never good practice to tell everything you know.

ABOUT THE AUTHOR

CAROLYN HART is the winner of multiple Agatha, Anthony, and Macavity Awards. She is a cofounder of Sisters in Crime. Her prolific career has included the enduring Death on Demand series as well as the Henrie O and Bailey Ruth books. At Malice Domestic, she received the 2012 Amelia Award and, in 2007, a Lifetime Achievement Award.